Rosemin Najmudin was born in Kamuli, Uganda, as was her father, and her three siblings. Her mum and eldest sister were born in Palitana, Gujerat, India. She has spent her life working in sustainable community development, health, teaching and lecturing. She published mainly in academia but also wrote children's stories and several short stories and chapters from recollection of her childhood. Many of her works have a focus on racism, faith, equality, gender and diversity as well as love and family.

Today she mainly works as a volunteer, and does some freelance work on global issues, health, diversity and sustainable environmental issues. She is now based in London, having travelled, lived and worked extensively throughout the world.

This book is dedicated to my parents, Mansur and Banu Najmudin. You were and are my inspiration. I never felt unloved and have always loved you.

Also for Kursum, Nurubhai (RIP), Shabir, Kurban, Faridabhabi, Zulfikar and Mubarakabhabi.

For Zainul Abedin, Sukayna, Zainub, Tasneem, Ibrahim and Shirin.

Always and forever, Adam Mansur, you know you are loved and you are the force behind everything I do.

Rosemin Najmudin

SHAFIQ AND TASNEEM – A MUSLIM LOVE STORY

AUSTIN MACAULEY PUBLISHERS™
LONDON • CAMBRIDGE • NEW YORK • SHARJAH

Copyright © Rosemin Najmudin 2023

The right of Rosemin Najmudin to be identified as author of this work has been asserted by the author in accordance with sections 77 and 78 of the Copyright, Designs and Patents Act 1988.

All rights reserved. No part of this publication may be reproduced, stored in a retrieval system, or transmitted in any form or by any means, electronic, mechanical, photocopying, recording, or otherwise, without the prior permission of the publishers.

Any person who commits any unauthorised act in relation to this publication may be liable to criminal prosecution and civil claims for damages.

This is a work of fiction. Names, characters, businesses, places, events, locales, and incidents are either the products of the author's imagination or used in a fictitious manner. Any resemblance to actual persons, living or dead, or actual events is purely coincidental.

A CIP catalogue record for this title is available from the British Library.

ISBN 9781398409538 (Paperback)
ISBN 9781398410589 (ePub e-book)

www.austinmacauley.com

First Published 2023
Austin Macauley Publishers Ltd®
1 Canada Square
Canary Wharf
London
E14 5AA

SHAFIQ

"You are terrified, fearful and scared. You have no idea why. You feel a deep sadness. Then you see them. You just see a person. This one person who makes everything bearable, the fear leaves and all the defeatist emotions dissipate. That is true love. All the negativity is replaced by immeasurable happiness and a calmness inside, instead."

Chapter 1
Dreams

I couldn't work out what was going on. I remembered Christmas; it had been so stressful and made me change the course of my history. I loved her and thought her parents loved me, well, her mother but not the siblings and definitely not their partners. This was England, I thought it a progressive and forward-thinking country. It was the twenty-first century. I had been proud to be British; I used to quietly laugh and be bored by discussions about racism, discrimination and inequality. I was amazed to hear people go on about it. I always thought it was their problem, their issue and always something blown out of all proportion. England was full of opportunity, I appreciated and valued the resources it offered, and all you had to do was work hard and do a good job to get on in life. I wasn't unsympathetic, I just felt that everyone was affected by some 'ism'; life had its downs as well as marvellous ups and the best way to bear it was just that. You had to rise above it, be better and stronger and in a position that no one could get to you. You just had to bear the bad and sad times. Of course, it hurt, but that only affected you and empowered them. If I heard the word 'racism', I usually left the discussion, the person or the party. It annoyed me and I found it irrelevant. It was only an issue if you chose to make it an issue, and my goodness, people like to share their stories, their insight, woes and play the violin pity party. People did like to go on.

I felt superior and righteous. I thought I always knew better; I was educated, was well read and, I suppose, I considered myself to be better informed. Knowledgeable. Problems existed for everyone; I had seen kids be nasty to each other for the slightest fault, and sometimes for no fault at all. I thought that racism was the same, if you consider yourself a victim, then people bullied you and only you suffer. The rest, and especially the perpetuator, just carried on, possibly happier that they had power over someone or had managed to hurt the person they never approved of in the first place.

I looked whiter than non-white. Some people thought of me as being Mediterranean, and a few considered me Arab as my name was very Islamic and I had their pale colouring. Of course, others loved to guess my background, was I mixed race, white and from another culture? This was another conversation I disliked. I was British. I was very proud of my heritage, but I never discussed it. I tanned easily and never needed sunblock. I loved to travel and loved learning about others and never ever felt the need to put people down or to judge them. I am sure I made mistakes, but I have never in my life turned away anyone who needed my help. In my work, I have met every type and kind of person, the ones who were so clean and polite, but tainted by illness, and others who had no care for anything or anyone, those who never washed and others who had no opportunity to wash because life had thrown them on a particular course. I met the wealthiest and the homeless, all needing the same help. Illness and sickness placed everyone on an even keel, even the rich and their money could not always buy the best healthcare, but money definitely helped. There were people who pushed their way to the top of the waiting list with their complaints and demands, but we tried hard to be fair and just in the work in the NHS; however, I made most of my own wealth by working in the private sector. I could have been righteous and put all my energy into my NHS work, but my compromise was that I earned a sober salary with the NHS. I refused bonuses and never charged extra for the long hours I often worked, even after I should have finished and gone home, I often stayed and fulfilled the extra demands by the NHS or if one cared enough to see through patients to the final course of their treatment. I know people thought me a snob and distant, but my patients never missed out on the very best care I was able to offer them, whether their treatment was paid by taxes or by their health insurance or from inherited wealth.

I heard them chatting in the kitchen. She referred to me as the Paki boyfriend, twice. I was actually her fiancé and not a 'Paki'. She had asked me to marry her and I thought the family were on our side.

Why am I dreaming of all this now?

I thought the family would be more honest and open. Do people not realise that if you gossip like this in a small family home, then someone is likely to hear you? Is this how they always talked when I wasn't there, did my fiancé join in? I thought I loved her, but this Christmas had not been the fun I expected. My Muslim family loved to celebrate Christmas, my goodness the food we all cooked and ate, the silly games played, and the laughter. Children took over the kitchen and their mums covertly advised, fussed, were stopped from taking over and gave their children all the credit even though they had done most of the prior preparations. It was insatiable; happiness flowed; there were arguments and tantrums, but the children made up, grudges from past family occasions came out, were discussed and were soon forgotten. They would be brought up again, no doubt about that! Did we gossip and put people down like this? I do not ever recall such blatant name-calling and rudeness of guests in my parents' home.

I had thought that Christmas in a British family home would be like the ones we saw on the television and on films. Full of hot chocolate with floating marshmallows, homemade biscuits and mince pies, the season of goodwill, friendship and joy. I honestly expected carols to be sung around the piano, my prospective mother-in-law actually played the piano really well, and she did play carols, but no one sang.

Everything was disappointing. It started like that and ended up being even worse. Mimi was unkind and inhospitable. We had arrived for brunch; they all knew I did not eat any meat from a pig as I had reminded Mimi to remind them more than once, yet they had made a full English breakfast. Sally said how she had grilled everything to make it healthy and only cooked the eggs in the bacon fat as it tasted so good. The whole house smelled of bacon when we arrived, of stale oil; the food was served on dishes kept warm, but everything was surrounded by bacon and pork sausages. There was talk about how wonderful it smelled and we were told to hurry up and come join in for the food. My fiancé, Mimi, no one called her Jasmine except me when it was just the two of us, did not say a word. I am polite, but I wasn't sure how to play this one. My mother-in-law remembered I was

Muslim and said to serve me only eggs, mushrooms, tomatoes and the fried bread. Sally was not stupid, and she hesitated as she could see all the food was close and touching in the one serving platter. Like her, I knew it was all cooked and splattered with the fat of meat I did not eat. I remember wondering how they would have treated me if I had been vegetarian? I thanked her but told her I was not hungry, and I hate to lie. So I excused myself by using the long drive and the horrendous traffic as an excuse for being tired. Mimi did speak and said she had slept the eight hours' drive to my family yesterday and then today we had met more traffic, such that instead of driving a total of six hours, I had been driving thirteen hours over the last two days. She told me to go to rest whilst she sat and piled her plate with food. I made some tea in the kitchen without asking and left them laughing and feasting.

I was hungry, starving as Mimi had told me that we would leave my family's home early as there would be lots to eat at her parent's home so I skipped the lavish breakfast at my parents' home. I put some biscuits in my pocket, took my mug of strong tea and went upstairs to the room in the attic. I sat on the lumpy mattress that had remained unchanged since Mimi was a child. This would be my bed over the next two nights. I would rest and then go downstairs to make things better. I could charm anyone.

My mum and two sisters cooked as they always do when it is the holidays, during family gatherings, and when we visited my parents' home first last night before we drove to Mimi's parents' home. They always worried about Mimi and had made all the food in double, so one had no chilli and less spice than the other identical dish so she would not be left out.

There were curries, homemade breads, salads, pickles, samosas, kebabs and a range of chutneys. They had also made a pasta bake and Lasagne in case she was sick of always eating curries at our home. There was Persian rice with saffron and crushed cardamom, soup and all kinds of food, but they still worried about making guests feel at home. Food is important, especially to my parents, both slim, but they love feeding the children, their families, grandchildren and visitors.

Although I was the oldest, I was the only one not yet married. They were happy that I had met Mimi and did not care about the cultural difference. I knew Mum preferred me to marry a girl who was at least a Muslim, but she accepted Mimi who was white and forthright when she first met my parents saying she was a staunch Atheist even though her family went to church. I had noticed she wrote her religion as 'Christian' when we filled forms. My family liked to watch people and get to know them before deciding on their character, were reserved and careful, but when any of the children brought people home, no questions were asked. They were welcomed, spoiled and treated like royalty.

My sister Remi was married to a lovely Muslim man, Rahim, she had met at university and they had been inseparable since. She had had a traditional wedding and was now a parent to two wonderful children. My youngest sister, Gulshan, was married and pregnant. All were happy that I brought a friend to meet them, and each time they met Mimi, they spoiled her and treated her with respect. Mimi was given a guest bedroom with an en suite. I noticed Mum had cleaned and polished the room; there were flowers in a vase and fresh towels laid out for Mimi. Presents had been left for Mimi on the bed. My sisters still asked if she had everything she needed. Mimi later whispered and asked me to sneak to her room, but I told her I couldn't do that as I respected my parents too much. This made her angry and sullen. I suffered with her silent treatment most of the long drive to her family home the next day for that. Instead of talking and keeping me company, especially when the traffic became heavy, she turned her head to look at the scenery outside. Soon I heard her quietly snoring, awaking as I pulled into her parents' home. Mimi did not forgive easily or quickly.

Mimi came up an hour later to check on me in her old bedroom, unchanged and more suited to a child than an adult guest. They had opened the prosecco we brought and she offered her glass to me so I could have a sip, but I shook my head to indicate I did not want any. I never really drank; I always had a glass to be sociable, but no one, not even Mimi, noticed that it never really got touched. When Mimi wasn't looking, I would pour it into her glass and get myself juice or soda water. Mimi was clearly angry, I could tell. She was trying to act normally, but she had that quiver of self-restraint, her eyes were shining and the pitch of her voice was slightly higher and not as it normally was. I knew her so well; I questioned how well she knew me and thought that she did not know me at all. She asked me how I was feeling but did not wait for an answer, then asked angrily why I was reading and not napping. She still didn't wait for me to speak; she then started to tell me how much effort she had made at my family's home and how disappointed she was with my rude behaviour today. I wanted to ask what that was, but I knew the signs. I knew that there had to be compromise, and I was a guest at her parents so I did not reply as an argument was brewing. Mimi had bought nothing for my family, except the flowers I had paid for in the M&S shop when we stopped at the service station to have a coffee after being caught in the terrible traffic. Her family had sent a list; they always did that each Christmas she had told me. Each child or guest brought a certain amount of booze and food as well as presents. We were asked to bring a joint of cooked beef, a cheese board, our own bedding and of course there were all the presents for everyone, wives and children included. I think I had spent about a thousand pounds on her family and another on her as she had not been shy to select a designer handbag and a Dior dress that she would wear on Christmas day. Yet she was angry because I would not eat an unhealthy breakfast splattered in pig fat. When had we ever gone out for such a breakfast and when had she ever seen me eat such food? The most I ever ate when we had breakfast outside our home was poached eggs, and occasionally, I might add some mushrooms and a tomato, but Mimi and I had never ever had such a fry-up. She had wanted to bring bacon to my flat, but I had refused her wish, and I told her that that was one area where I would not compromise. I would not allow any products from a pig into my home, not even for her.

This was pretty much how the next two days went. I was quiet, conversations stopped when I entered a room or sat next to one of Mimi's family. I felt that her mother was the only one who was polite and made polite conversation with me. The food was awful; Mimi's father cooked the Christmas dinner, and he forgot and covered the turkey in bacon so I could not eat that on Christmas day nor the potatoes lying next to the bacon. He told me to take the bacon off and eat the turkey. I just couldn't. Mimi stared at me in quiet anger. I smiled at her, and she looked away. I had a plate full of slightly over-cooked bland vegetables for my Christmas dinner. I have no idea what happened to the cooked joint of beef I had brought.

Another dream took me to a work meeting. We had gone to Cafe Rouge for lunch. I hadn't been hungry, but three of my colleagues insisted I come and have lunch with them. I was really busy and never relished going out at lunchtime as there were queues and never enough time to choose, order and eat the food in an enjoyable way. They decided that we should all have pizzas, and I made sure the waitress understood that mine was without the ham, and she said did I want mushrooms instead, and I nodded. The pizzas all came out the same, all with prosciutto ham. I called the waitress and one of my colleagues interrupted and said there was no time, why didn't I just pick the ham off, and I could even give it to him. The waitress took my pizza away, and she returned with the exact same pizza with the ham removed, and I could see what she had done as there were clear spaces showing where the prosciutto ham had been. I never got angry; no one at the table said anything; I had eaten nothing, and they had all finished. They got ready to leave, told me to get a sandwich and settle the bill. They left me on my own and said they would pay me later.

Liberal, inclusive, tolerant and transparent UK of the twenty-first century. Mimi and I didn't last; she cried and cried when I told her that I wasn't happy. I apologised and said I did not want to marry her, but she replied that she didn't understand why I was so unhappy in our relationship. She told me it was normal to have ups and downs, that I expected too much from her and she kept crying and asking me why. Did she forget our first Christmas with her family a few months ago? I had tried to talk to her about how I had felt each week after week, before I could bear it no longer and I had asked her to leave. Every time I tried to talk to her, how I felt during that awful Christmas, when I told her about being called Paki and she would turn to face me with that look. I hated that look. Scorn, disbelief, anger and then the way she spoke to me or hours and days of silent treatment. No one had treated me like that; she made me feel stupid, worthless and that I was the problem. I told her that I had never felt or experienced racism and how in the past I had ignored people who tried to talk to me about racism. She asked if I was calling her family racist, did not wait for me to answer, but she put her coat on and left, slamming the door. She had said that she loved me and I could tell her anything in the heady days when we first met. Words. I did not see her for a week; her best friend came the next day and took a case of her clothes. She knew I was in my flat, but she let herself into my home, went into the bedroom and did not greet me or knock and ask if it was all right for her to go into my bedroom. For me, this was the final seal on our end.

Mimi came back a week later, said nothing and got into our bed. I pretended to be asleep. The next few days, I worked late, slept in my office and spent the weekend at my parents'. I had left her a letter to explain how I felt. I did not blame her nor mention her family, but for me the relationship was over and I needed her to take her things and leave my home. She didn't try to talk to me; she rarely sent me texts anyway and never called after the letter. I couldn't bear being this unhappy. I didn't even need to talk to my family about it, they just knew. They knew me and could see how miserable I was. Why was Mimi not like this? Why didn't she understand or at least try to see things from my perspective? Why did she not listen to me?

I love my wife; she gave me what I had never realised that I longed for, and I love my two sons. Mimi had confirmed to me that I should remain a bachelor and that I was not cut out for marriage. Tasneem made me want to live, and she pushed me to fight. She knew that I could always hear her, and she fought everyone when they wanted to turn the machines off that were keeping me alive.

I don't know what is real and what are my dreams. I can smell her perfume; I bought her Chanel and Pablo Picasso, but she uses the attar, the lovely traditional Muslim scent my mum gave her as one of her wedding gifts and now I have to buy her more every time she starts to run out. My mum liked Mimi, but I know she loves Tasneem. I hear Mum and Tasneem talking; I want to scream, "I can hear you!" Tasneem's mum, her dad and Popa arrived. They all talk to me and talk to each other. I can hear them recite prayers, and I can smell the food they are eating. So many times, I hear a nurse come and tell them off for eating in my room, but they have never stopped. I am glad. I love the smells. I loved Tasneem more than ever. Was that possible? I knew I had fallen in love with her almost the first time I met her.

I thought I loved Mimi. Did I, had I loved her? Most of my life, I had focused on work, and I thought I would never marry. To be honest, I thought myself incapable of love. Of course I dearly loved my family, but loving a woman? I doubted it. My parents kept suggesting an arranged marriage, but it did not have any appeal for me. Then Mimi walked in. I rarely went to parties, but I was forced to go to my old roommate's engagement party. Tim and I had shared a room when we were doing our residency at Addenbrookes Hospital in Cambridge; it was a hectic time of long shifts, little sleep, and yet we had become close as housemates. He worked hard and often told me about the poverty he experienced as a child which had made him want to succeed and do well in life. He had loved school in his small village in Scotland, done well and got into Edinburgh University to study medicine even though none of his family had done well academically. He moved to England as there was more opportunity here and that is when I met him. He loved to read, liked the odd drink, but he was unlike most of the students I had met on my courses who ended up in the pub at every opportunity. Tim was gentle, widely read and I knew he sent home any spare money he had. Even as a junior doctor, he worked at bars and restaurants when he had any spare time. On our very little time off, we hiked, walked around the beautiful city of Cambridge and I had even got him interested in cricket!

When Tim and I went out socially, we went with Simon, Puleen and Gita. Simon was a Commonwealth scholarship student who came from Uganda, Puleen was a Hindu Indian born in Kenya and Gita was also a Hindu from West London; her parents were born in India but had started a business in Somalia and moved to London in the late 1960s when Somalia was ravaged by civil unrest and war. We always joked that Tim was the ethnic minority in our little group and wondered why there was no indigenous English person in our party? On days off, we either cooked and ate together, explored the countryside around us or visited one of the quaint villages surrounding Cambridge. I was the only one with a car as my mum had given me her old car which she wanted to have scrapped, but I begged to have it as it was so old I could afford the car insurance on it. Popa wanted to buy me a better car, but I was more independent and stubborn in those days so I refused his help. We also all loved music and Cambridge was a great place to work; we went to local gigs, camped at festivals in the summer sharing an old tent and cooking on a fire.

They all loved the food my family always sent me, particularly Tim and Simon as they had no real family in England. Tim was close to his family, but it was too expensive for him to visit home often as he was from Scotland so he really liked it when my parents came to see me, bringing my sisters or cousins or any of the other family. He shared in their love and quickly became part of my family. He had fallen in love with both my sisters, and we teased the three of them about it all the time as it was a mutual crush rather than anything serious as we had all met Rahim who was dating Remi. We always invited him to share our food or he came out with us when we ate in a restaurant that popa always invited us to and paid for. Over the years, he had popped in to see me, also visited my parents' home and was chuffed when they asked him to stay for dinner.

Tim made me promise to come to his engagement party as he had already asked me to be his best man at the wedding that was happening the following year. I liked his fiancé, Fiona, who was also from Scotland, and the wedding was to be back home. So, I had no choice but to attend his engagement party, and as soon as I entered, I snuck out onto the balcony and decided I would go in shortly to talk to Tim and Fiona before I made my excuses and left. I had had a long, busy day at work and all I liked to do on a Friday night was see one of my siblings, and if I wasn't working over the weekend, I loved driving to see my parents. I got the third degree interrogation from all of them every time I visited; there would always be an initial mention of some girl looking for a husband, and I would look at the photograph and see if there was something there, a glimmer, to make me want to actually meet them. I never saw or felt that 'something special' or any sparks.

Mimi came onto the balcony; it was weeks later that she told me that she wanted a sneaky cigarette, and had I known that we definitely would not have dated. I am as anti-smoking as they get, being a surgeon, I have seen too many lungs ravaged by smoking or cancers caused by heavy smokers. Instead of lighting her cigarette, Mimi started to talk to me. I had never been able to talk to any woman that easily, except for my sisters. Mimi teased, flirted and got me to talk. We were there for almost an hour until I noticed her starting to shiver, and we went inside to talk to the others, find a drink and get a snack. We chatted to Tim and Fiona and then left. I offered to drop Mimi home, but she said she didn't live far and wanted to walk home. I watched her go after we exchanged mobile numbers.

I saw her almost every day for the next three weeks. She would come to the hospital to meet me for a quick coffee, or she would come at the end of the evening and we would go for dinner. We met at galleries and museums; we walked and talked. She often hinted that she wanted to come back to my flat, but this was too soon for me. She asked me if I would be her plus one for a weekend gathering with her friends in ten days' time and I agreed. She said that her battery had almost run out and asked if we could check the hotel on my phone, and we booked a hotel room for two nights. I had my credit card details stored in my phone and so paid for the hotel without being asked.

Everyone assumed that I had been with many women over the years I was single, even though no one ever saw me with anyone. I did not tell Mimi that I had never been intimately close to a woman; she knew that I had never had a long-term girlfriend, but she assumed, like everyone else, rather than asked me if I had slept with many women. We had arrived at the hotel in time for dinner on Friday night of her friends' gathering, and it was a noisy, rowdy night. I saw a totally different side to Mimi; she drank a lot of alcohol, was loud and went outside with various friends to have a cigarette and was quite flirty with everyone she met. I liked to dance, but am quite shy. Mimi pulled her friends to the dance floor, but never asked me to dance with her so I was locked in seats next to people I hardly knew and sat quietly, listening to others talking around me. At about eleven o'clock, I kissed her goodnight and said I was going up to the room.

I showered and got into bed. She woke me at about 2 am. She was in her underwear and was trying to make love to me. I was dressed in my pyjamas, and she was trying to undress me. It was horrible; she smelled of alcohol and cigarettes and had not even showered. She was rough and awkward. I felt a little scared, uncomfortable and wasn't sure what to do. She was so drunk; she eventually burped and fell asleep on top of me. I gently moved her to the side and covered her up.

I couldn't get her to wake up the next morning from her deep slumber and thunderous snoring. I went down for breakfast and saw her friends arrive as I was ready to leave the dining room; they waved to me, and I smiled. I decided to go for a walk. Mimi woke up about midday; she was very hungover and called me on my mobile to ask me to return to our room. I noticed that she had thrown up in the bathroom and hadn't cleaned it properly. She got up and showered. She said that we would drive to the sea and lunch had been organised in a restaurant near the sea. I smiled in acceptance and watched her nurse the strong coffee she was drinking.

She moved into my flat three months later, and I don't remember how that happened. I had never asked her to; after the weekend with her friends, she knocked on my door a few days later. She stayed that night and the next night. When I was at a work conference one weekend, she was at the flat when I got back; she had asked the concierge to let her in, and she had put some of her clothes in my wardrobe. We went to meet both our families that Christmas a month later to tell them of our engagement. I couldn't exactly tell you how it had happened that we were to get married. We had seen my family a few times, but I had only briefly met her parents once, and I spoke to one of two of her siblings when they called on my house phone, but had never met them until that Christmas.

I arrived at my home after seeing my parents. I didn't tell them anything, but Mum noticed I did not look well and told me she was worried. They promised to come and stay with me soon, and I told them how much I would love that; they had come once before, but it was hard for them to find me living with Mimi and wanted me to formalise the arrangement. I told them I wasn't ready, but Mimi had wanted the same thing as my parents. She asked me to marry her. We had only been together a few months, and I was surprised to even hear her talking about marriage. I just wasn't ready, but it seemed wrong to say 'No!' She had gone down on one knee, asked me to marry her, and I lifted her up and she asked me for an answer as she faced me, so I replied, 'Yes, of course!' I did tell her she had taken me by surprise and that it would please my parents, but I wanted to wait at least a year before we married. I thought she had been a good listener; however, all I heard her talk about to her family and friends after the proposal was about the impending wedding. I was so worried, but as with difficult things and past moments, I needed time, I just could not voice clearly what I was feeling, share my fears and precisely what I wanted. I also feared Mimi's reaction.

I couldn't open the door to my flat when I returned from visiting my parents; I tried again and peeked into the lock to see what was wrong and noticed the lock was different, new and shiny. Mimi had the locks changed, why? This was my home, my flat. I hadn't ever asked her to pay a penny towards anything when she moved in. I had a cleaner who came twice each week so she didn't need to do an iota of work when she lived with me; the shopping was ordered online and the concierge brought it in and my cleaner put everything away. I called the concierge and asked him if he had the keys to my flat, and he said he had seen Mimi get the locks changed, but she had not yet given him a set of keys. I rang the intercom and called Mimi on her mobile. She didn't answer, and there was no voicemail to leave a message. What was going on?

It took me thirteen months and a cost of over twenty thousand pounds in solicitor's fees to get my home back. I wanted to walk away, but my family refused to let Mimi get away with such bad behaviour. When I finally got to enter my home I noticed she took my paintings, anything of value and had poured paint on some of my clothes, my sofa and Persian rug when she had eventually been forced to leave.

When I went to the solicitor who tried to use mediation to sort out the relationship breakdown with Mimi, she emailed my employers and told them that I had abused her and there was a police investigation about this. I would have been suspended from work, but I had been with the same NHS hospital and the same partners in my private work, so each checked with the police and found that Mimi was lying. The police visited her as they had the email evidence sent to my employers, but she wouldn't let them into the flat and did not attend the police interview at the station.

My solicitor got a possession order for my flat, but she still would not leave. I had to get bailiffs involved, and eventually, they broke into my flat. Mimi had already been to the flat the day before with her father and a van. None of us had expected this and when the concierge called me, it was too late to stop them taking all my precious things; the painting was from my parents when I graduated from medical school. She took the cufflinks that had belonged to my grandfather and the dinner set that belonged to my mum's family in Tehran. I remembered how Mum let all of us unwrap the dinner set for special dinners, telling us stories about her childhood in Persia. We would always correct her and say it was now called Iran, but she always used the old name. Mum had shared out her dinner set amongst her children, but when my sisters' children came along, the set was given to me as the nominated grown-up to look after it intact. I had once shared this with Mimi, how it belonged to all three of us. She had not only stolen from me but also from my sisters and parents as well. My family and friends who had been kind to her and loved her just because she was with me and she repaid all of us in this petty and cruel way.

We had been to Iran twice. I was always planning to take Mum again, but work was all-consuming, and I knew that I would take her as soon as I was better. I rarely talked or told people about my Iranian background. I often questioned if I dreamed what I was telling them. I was even more confused right now. Memories were so blurred, I remembered my nanna, Mum's father perfectly, but I was five years old when I saw him before he passed away. Stories Mum had told us were getting confused within my dreams and actual facts. I had clear visions of him, of Nanna playing cricket in the backyard, yet when we had gone to see him, he was a dying and frail man who had never left his bed, I had never actually seen him play cricket, and it was days later before we were attending his funeral. What was going on, why was I dreaming like this?

I woke up and found I was in the hospital theatre; Tasneem was next to me. This was clearly a dream as we have never worked together and absolutely never operated together. I also see that it is Mum in the operating theatre; I am so afraid and screaming, but I hear hushed whispers. Tasneem is talking to Mum about her first birth, why are they talking about that in the hospital theatre? What on earth is going on?

I loved being an uncle, but never expected to have children. Mimi had told me early on that she felt there were too many people on our Earth, and she had no maternal feelings either, so she did not want to have children. This had disappointed me, devastated me in actual fact, but like everything with her, I just accepted it and said nothing. I realise now that we never actually discussed and agreed on anything. She controlled me and made the decisions. I was simply her provider for the type of life she had always hoped for, dinners out, expensive presents and weekends away. I remember being exhausted one week and wanting to rest; but she had planned and booked a cottage inviting some friends of her. I told her that I always visited my family when my parents or a family member had a birthday, but instead we were in Scotland when Popa turned sixty, and I know how much this had hurt my parents. I thought that she would have invited Tim and Fiona, but it was the same friends of hers I had met throughout our relationship. I had not managed to get close to any of them. To be honest, they were not the kind of people I usually associated with. Mimi told me she had packed for me, but she had forgotten to pack my coat, and I had frozen the three days we were away whilst she and her friends went walking and hiking, leaving me alone when all I longed for was to be with my family. I had paid for all of this and hated every moment. I became agitated; I heard Tasneem call the nurse, even though she could manage the equipment herself. I had never seen her panic like this in all the years we have been together. I could hear the fear in her voice. I shouted, "Tasneem!"

I had never asked Mimi why she was at Tim and Fiona's engagement party, assuming that she was their close friend as they hadn't invited a lot of people. This was one of the things I liked about Mimi, if she was their close friend, then she had to be a decent person. Tim didn't want a stag party; I teased him and asked if he was really Scottish, but he fitted none of the stereotypes. He and Fiona were happy to have a cosy and intimate dinner, instead, the month before their wedding, with four other close friends that included me. Tim had booked a West End restaurant that included a show. The food was delicious; the show and a comedy act made us laugh, especially when we heckled the comedian by telling them that Tim and Fiona were about to get married, so the comedian picked on them, but in a jovial and cheeky way. The night ended with dancing. It was such an easy night of doing fun dances, chatting and generally catching up with each other's news. We all knew each other over the ten years of our personal growth and career development, so there was ease and trust. We would all meet again at the wedding and this was a lovely way to start the celebrations.

The next day, I had driven us down to see my parents with Tim and Fiona and were sitting in the garden having chai and snacks. My two sisters were coming later with their families for a garden party or a barbeque. I hadn't worried or got involved and instead let them all plan whatever they wanted to do. These were my favourite weekends. It was during this meeting that Tim teased and asked me what had happened to the girl I had met on his balcony? I asked them how they knew Mimi, and it turned out that they didn't know her at all. She was a friend of a friend's and had arrived at their flat uninvited. Tim and Fiona were busy as they had decided to move back to Scotland so we hadn't talked until now. They had just come back for a short break to London, stayed with me and we had come to have this gathering with my family. It was only then many of the doubts I had surfaced. I told Tim about how things had progressed with Mimi, and he confirmed that she was not the close friend I assumed she was. Both he and Fiona felt devastated about what happened and felt enormous guilt that they had been complicit in our meeting each other, but I could be honest with them. It wasn't their fault at all. It was Mimi who had acted the way she had and done the awful things she had decided and chosen to do. No one else was to blame, certainly never Tim and Fiona.

Gulshan arrived and ran to Tim and Fiona. We started to tease her about how she would cope now that Tim, her first love, was getting married. Fiona was aware of all the jokes, and she made a face of disapproval until Gulshan pulled her up, put her arm in Fiona's and the two women walked off to have a gossip. Fiona had quickly become close to my family, and as only women can do, was now part of the gang that I failed to always understand and be a part of.

Tim loved my family and had said he wanted all of us to come to Scotland for his wedding, but instead only I was attending with my parents. We knew he meant it, but the wedding was quite small with family and few friends, so we had not wanted to take over. We, my parents and I instead had decided to make a short holiday of it, so we took flights to Edinburgh and hired a car. We stayed in a hotel on the way to Fiona's home town. The wedding was wonderful; it was intimate, yet there were enough people for a ceilidh. It was just over an hour from Edinburgh, so we stopped on the outskirts of Edinburgh and spent a day walking around the wonderful city. We drove to the hotel Tim had insisted on paying for our stay. The wedding was at 3 pm, and we arrived at the hotel at 10 am as a short walk was organised for guests to get to know each other. We loved this. We caught up with the few friends we had met in London, but the rest of the guests were new to us, yet all treated us as if we were their long-lost friends. Scottish culture is not dissimilar to that of our culture! Lunch was simple, soup, fresh bread and cheese.

We went to bathe and dress; the church was walking distance from the hotel. I had already gone to see Tim, and we had a coffee together before he joined everyone on the walk. Fiona was busy getting ready. I left my parents to get ready, whilst I went to help Tim; he dressed in a kilt and looked amazing. He had asked if I wanted to wear a kilt, but I joked I would be happier in my designer suit! Tim had chosen to be a GP rather than enter the competitive world of hospitals as I had done, and although we were both successful, it was clear from the start that my wealth exceeded his.

We were the only non-Scottish guests, even his friends in London were from Scotland, but we were treated so well. The church was beautiful; it was about two hundred and fifty years old. I imagine it must be freezing and draughty in the winter, but on this warm day, it was a stunning and peaceful place to get married. The wedding ceremony was relaxed and touching, vows were said and a few jokes were made. I didn't mean to do the silly thing of forgetting their rings, but I had asked my parents to look after them as I was running around doing last minute arrangements for Tim and had forgotten this. So when they asked for the rings, I really could not find them in any of my pockets! Popa got up to give me the rings, Tim turned around and said he knew he should have made him my best man instead of me. Everyone laughed and he winked at me. Photographs were taken by family and friends; there was nothing overly showy and pretentious; the wedding reflected Tim and Fiona's characters, honest, beautiful and down to earth.

The reception was also walking distance from the church, and I was glad that Mimi was not the close friend I had assumed she was to Tim and Fiona so had not been invited to their wedding. We walked to the reception held at the back of our hotel in a marquee. There was a buffet and the music started immediately. This time, there was alcohol available and some people made the most of it, but Tim had organised mocktails for us, and we were given elegant glasses decorated with fruit and edible flowers. The food was light; there was seafood and locally sourced salmon and trout; there were salads and vegetables and different desserts. We ate, chatted to the various guests who all came to tell us how stunning Mum looked in her traditional clothes; she had chosen to wear a saree Popa had given her about fifteen years earlier. It was very simple but embroidered and with sequins that caught the occasional sunshine and looked like flecks of tiny diamonds caught and floating in the air. Popa and Mum were happy and joined in with all the chatter, dancing and storytelling. Both of my parents were pulled onto the dance floor to do the group ceilidh dances, and even I joined in. The only time I missed not having a partner was at English weddings as they seemed to be made for couples and families, but this wedding was more like an Asian wedding. You had to participate and no one minded if you were alone or not; the whole occasion was inclusive and so much fun.

There was a break in the ceremony for speeches and thanks; I never struggled at public speaking, and it wasn't hard to praise Tim, and I was even able to tell stories about Fiona as I had known the couple ever since they had met in London. Guests clapped and cheered when I told witty stories about this wonderful couple. I was heckled and the guests joined in. What I loved was that in Scotland both of the couple said a few words and this part of the wedding ended with Tim thanking everyone, then Fiona ending the speeches. She mentioned her love for Tim but also for all the people who had attended, her family, Tim's family; she mentioned my parents and I, how we had been their surrogate family when they lived in London. It was all touching and kind. I saw tears around Mum's eyes. Then the younger guests joked and told them to get it finished as their feet were itching to dance, so after a final toast, the simply decorated, but splendid wedding cake was cut and the dancing began again. This time, there was more popular music intercepted with ceilidh music. My parents left at about 11 pm and refused my offer to walk them to their hotel room, but I saw that Tim made sure one of his cousins made sure they got to their room safely. I stayed until the end of the night, people would come up to chat, and I was constantly pulled onto the dance floor. It was a great wedding. Tim and Fiona were staying in the same hotel; they had been living together for at least five years, so there was no fuss made about their first night together. We saw them the next day at another walk, this time organised for a small number of close family and us after a drive to the nearby sea. The wind was cold and strong, but after a brisk walk and a tour with some stories about local histories, we had a beautiful picnic in an old ruined castle. We played frisbee as my parents chatted with older members of the couple's family as they watched us being silly, playful and childish.

We ate in the town that night. There were about three tables booked for close family, and we were included in this group. We played musical chairs all night with people moving around and chatting to each other. I saw Popa and Mum, each happy and alone away from the other most of the night chatting to various different people and occasionally coming together as if they needed to share the notes they had each taken. How I wished I had this or even what Tim and Fiona had, but I felt I would never have this. I did not feel at all sad, the time in Scotland was so fun, and it made me realise my life was exactly as it should be.

We were flying back to London after the wedding from Glasgow and again had booked a hotel on the way to the airport near one of the Lochs. Tim and Fiona flew to France early that day so we all watched them being driven off by one of their friends who would drop them at the airport. We left soon after, waving goodbye and with jokes that we would see them all again at the christening of the first child of the newly married couple.

How different this trip was to that I had experienced with Mimi and her friends during our last visit to Scotland! I don't think I had been alone for this period of time on holiday with my parents since I had been a child. I loved my sisters, but I had also needed this. I felt that my soul was being cleansed, refuelled and was on the road to recovery.

We hired a boat to investigate the Loch once we had found our rooms in the hotel and had some tea. It was a little cooler today, but with warm coats, it was a pleasant morning on the wide span of water. We had eaten so much over the last few days; we sat on the banks and ate some quiche with salad and fruit. Mum had asked the hotel staff to prepare a flask of tea with the simple picnic, which was a great idea. They left me lost in my thoughts, and I was happy skimming flat stones on the calm Loch waters. I returned and found Popa was dozing, so Mum and I chatted quietly. I loved our closeness. I smiled as I looked at both of them and Mum gave me an enquiring look, though I am sure she agreed that we had such a good relationship. She always talked about how blessed our life was. She had everything she wanted and ever hoped for, and she wished this for all her children.

Mimi and I had never actually argued about anything. What usually happened was that she liked to organise our lives; she always wanted us to do everything together, always with her friends and this was simply not possible. I had work commitments; she got angry if I was late, but my operations on patients were unpredictable, and they over ran or I would be called to go to attend to a patient in the middle of the night. This would result in her giving me the silent treatment until she needed something from me. I soon realised that when she was in a good mood, she wanted something from me or had her friends visiting, and I heard her brag to them about various things. These days, it was always about the wedding, where she hoped to have it and her ideas of where we might go on honeymoon. I knew nothing about any of this as we had never discussed any of it. I learned most about our lives when we met, visited or had her friends visit us. After we got engaged, she did not want to come to my family gatherings or to visit my parents or sisters. She made an excuse, made alternative arrangements for us and like with Popa's birthday, I would miss key family gatherings and this really upset me. I knew I was very unhappy, but did not know how to resolve the situation easily and without both of us getting upset. My dreams were turning into nightmares.

Chapter 2
The Fountain of Paradise

Dr Tasneem worked in paediatrics and had come to find me because she had a child from Malaysia who needed specialised and innovative treatment that was only available in the UK. The hospital could not get her the help needed on the NHS; we often bent the rules, but not in this special case. There were too many experts, specialist resources and requiring a lengthy theatre slot that involved costs which could not be hidden from the bureaucratic accountants. She had gone through the hospital staff list and tried to identify staff who could help her raise funds and recognised I was Muslim from my name. Dr Tasneem knocked on my door, did not wait for me to answer and walked into my office. She introduced herself and sat down across from me. She was like a cyclone; fast, busy and quietly frantic. She told me about the child called Umayma who was seven years old and the treatment she urgently needed. Told me how the hospital was unable to give her what she needed for free. She needed help to raise the money, a very huge amount, and that she had asked several mosques to fundraise for the child and they willingly agreed to help raise cash for her treatment, but they were short of a few thousand pounds. She asked me if someone from my community or mosque could help. She told me she understood I was busy and would leave it with me, so she got up and left. She made me smile; she was gentle, beautiful, intelligent yet assertive. I had never met anyone quite like her. I wondered why I had never seen her before, but I realised that I was not very sociable, and I rushed from one hospital to the next, from patient to patient. I was very busy, and when I wasn't working, I liked to go home or to be with my family. Also the hospital was huge, full of specialist areas, endless corridors, several floors, and I had no cause or concern to ever visit the majority of them.

I only went to the mosque for Eid-ul-Fitr, the festival at the end of Ramadan and this was really only to appease my mum. I hated the hierarchy in Islam and the pretend-patriarchy at the mosque as we were a type of Islam where all the family, including the women and children, went to the main section of the mosque. Even when it was clear that it was the women who actually managed the smooth running of the beautiful mosque, built to look like any of the great mosques around the Muslim world, it was often the men who took all the credit. This did not happen, I hope, in my family.

I had returned early one morning two days later to the NHS hospital to find a note pinned on my door from Dr Tasneem reminding me about the urgency of raising the money for Umayma. I called her, but she did not answer, so I texted her to ask for the amount of money she still needed, and she sent me a reply within minutes after apologising for not answering my call and saying she was very busy. I called Mum and told her about Umayma, asked if she knew anybody who might be able to help and told her that Dr Tasneem thought we should ask for support from our mosque. My mum asked me how much money they still needed, and I gave her a rough estimate. Mum asked me for the bank details and mum asked me to leave it with her. I called Dr Tasneem, got her voicemail, so I left Mum's mobile number, and asked her to talk to mum directly as she had some ideas to raise the remaining money she needed quickly. Mum had sent the remaining funds to Dr Tasneem using her own savings within the hour and Umayma had her operation later that day instead of having to wait a week or so for the remaining donation needed. I had not known any of this.

Dr Tasneem came and found me locking the door later that day. She looked exhausted. I told her that I still had to see some patients, but was ready for a short break. She asked if I had time for a quick cup of tea as she wanted to update me, and I opened my office as I had everything to make her a cup of chai. She was surprised to find I drank chai. I placed a tin of shortbread and some snacks Mum had given me in a stainless-steel container as she knew I often didn't have time to eat. Dr Tasneem ate gratefully and helped herself, in between telling me all about Umayma's operation, and she told me that my mum had helped her raise all the funds needed quickly. I said I would try to visit her the next day. Dr Tasneem told me all about how she had met Umayma, how she had managed to get the airlines to give two free tickets for Umayma and her mother to come to London, how helpful the Malaysian Embassy had been and how ill the child was. She would have died within the month had they not operated. It had taken six and a half hours in the operating theatre, but so far everything looked good. I offered Dr Tasneem some more snacks, and Dr Tasneem said to call her by her name and drop the 'Dr'. She hadn't had time to eat lunch that day, but restrained herself even though I told her to help herself to more. She shook her head and said she would save herself for her mum's food. We got up and walked out together. I offered her a lift, but she went for her bicycle, and I returned and went to see my patients. Why had I offered her a lift? I hadn't even finished my work! It was totally impractical. I just liked spending time with her already.

I was called away to an urgent case the next day and did not manage to see Umayma, and it was a week later when I realised I had not managed to visit the child. Mum wanted to come and see her, and after she called to ask how she was, I told her I hadn't managed to see Umayma, and I heard the disapproval in her voice. She made me promise to see her so after my rounds, I popped into the children's ward. In all my years at this hospital, I had never been here, at the children's ward. Why was this ward so joyous, colourful and relaxed, whilst adult wards seemed to be full of stress and beigeness? Umayma was awake and her mother greeted me and kissed the back of my hand when I introduced myself as Dr Shafiq. I was embarrassed, could not explain much to her because of language barriers and that I was not Umayma's surgeon. A nurse came and I asked her for an update. Umayma was doing really well, what a beautiful child, she was playing with some toys and chatting to her mum. She had stopped talking when I came into her room, but gave me a wide smile, and I saw she had a tooth missing. I video-called Mum, introduced her to Umayma and her mum and told them this was my mum. Don't ask me how they did this, but the two women and child managed to talk to each other without having a language in common, used signs and there were giggles and tears. I stood and watched, hoping Dr Tasneem might have come. My phone was returned to me fifteen minutes later.

Mum arrived and visited the next day with a basket full of food, some clothes for mother and daughter, more toys, books and with a Malaysian friend of hers who translated for them. Mum stayed until the nurse came and told her Umayma needed to rest. Mum invited Umayma and her mum to stay with her when they were ready to leave the hospital, but Umayma could not be moved for a few weeks and then she was to be an outpatient so had to be quite near to the hospital. Tasneem had found a Malaysian family near the hospital to host them while Umayma recovered. Mum asked why her husband was not there, but they had two other children and a business so he had to stay behind. Tasneem had told me about the huge costs involved; she had only managed to get two free tickets and did not want to waste money on flights in case they needed it to pay for Umayma's treatment. Also, their in-laws, the grandparents, lived with them so it would have been too much for both of Umayma's parents to come to London. Mum would have offered to pay his ticket had she known, but instead, she nodded in understanding and visited every week until Umayma was discharged. Mum had met Dr Tasneem a few times, and they got on immediately.

I went to see Umayma on her last day in the hospital. Whilst she was recovering, she had become a popular little thing; she had picked up English very quickly and was liked by all. She rarely complained about her pain and the discomfort we all knew she was experiencing. Dr Tasneem had told me how much pain she must have been in. She had started to gain weight, but she was extremely tiny and thin for her age, though her mum was petite and I imagined she would never get to be all that big. Her mum kissed my hand again and Umayma gave me a huge hug when I gave her a children's book I had bought her. Mum could not come on that day, and sweet Umayma told me how she loved my mummy and looked forward to seeing her. Children are so quick to love. She was still struggling to digest food and left the hospital still wearing her feeding tube, but it was lovely to see her in a dress, walking and holding her mother's hand. Dr Tasneem stood next to me and asked if I had time for lunch; she apologised that she had no food from her mum to share, and we went to the hospital canteen. She insisted on paying, again mentioning the need to thank me even when I tut-tutted her. She had seen my large donation I had made on the JustGiving fundraising page even before my mum had given her the remaining sum of money needed for the surgery. I was sure I had made it secretly, so how had she found out? She asked me a lot of questions, and we chatted until my beeper went off, over an hour had passed and I said goodbye without needing to explain.

Popa came and picked them up before they left London to return to Malaysia so that they could spend two days with them in their home and meet the family. Umayma was totally recovered; the feeding tubes were gone and she chattered with my nieces and nephews. I saw them briefly at my parents' home, before Popa and Mum dropped them to the airport, where Dr Tasneem waited to say goodbye to them. I had only managed to pop in and say goodbye to Umayma and her mother, but it was clear a bond had been formed between all of us. Mum had bought them a suitcase which she filled with presents, asked Umayma's mother what they needed by using her Malaysian friend as translator, and Mum had taken her shopping and had brought them everything they needed without making them feel embarrassed. My mum had this easy, kind and generous nature that she had passed onto all her children. She was so good at putting people at ease and never regretted anything she did. Both my parents spoke of their luck at the good life they had, always wanted to share their fortune and I could see that life really was what you made it.

I kept seeing Dr Tasneem from a distance when I was in the hospital. She always waved and smiled, but she was always rushing and forever busy. She passed my office a few times to deliver food her mum had made. She told me she didn't know how else to thank me, even though I said I had done nothing and it had been my mum, but Tasneem reminded me that it was me who had introduced my mum to them. Her mum was a great cook. Sometimes she dropped the food and rushed off, but the best times were when she stayed a while and chatted as we shared and ate lunch together. She had told me her parents were from India and East Africa, but she had been born in London. I didn't know then, but she had seen and chatted to my mum a few times and the two women got on famously and were now friends, often chatting and messaging each other.

I hardly recognised Dr Tasneem at a management meeting, this was the first time she was not in scrubs. She waved when she saw me, but continued to chat to her colleague. She was extremely pretty, and I had never noticed how much so and how I liked seeing her. She had flowing, thick dark brown hair, eyes to match that were surrounded by faint laugh lines and she was much slimmer than I realised. I wondered about her age and whether she was married; I looked at her hands and there were no rings. I had to wait until the end of the meeting to chat to her; she came up to me, introduced two colleagues and we walked out together. We were invited to the pub, and both Dr Tasneem and I said 'No' in unison, smiles lighting our faces. I said I was tired and Dr Tasneem said her mum was waiting for her. I offered her a lift and she accepted much to my amazement after telling me off yet again for calling her Dr Tasneem. She lived fifteen minutes away. I asked her where her bicycle was and she said it needed servicing so her father was doing it, but he needed to buy some parts so she thought she would have to take the bus home that night, and she teased by saying she was happy to be in my posh and expensive car instead. She never let up! She lived in a quiet cul-de-sac with her parents and siblings; she had a sister Tara and a brother Ali Asgar. She was the eldest and bemoaned the fact that all her family and relatives had been trying to get her married for the last ten years. She told me she had seen about twenty men to date, pharmacists, factory workers, men who owned shops and one who was a millionaire, but none had the qualities she was looking for. When we arrived at her home, she politely invited me in, but I shook my head and told her I had an early start the next day. I thanked her for her delightful company, winked at her and said goodnight instead. I hoped I hadn't been too standoffish.

    I didn't see her for ten days. When I did see her, she smiled, and I actually felt a relief in my heart. She was rushing as always, but I followed her, and she told me they were short staffed so she had been very busy, missing meals and had tried to visit Umayma as often as she could after work or at the weekend. She asked how I was but did not wait for me to answer as a nurse came to ask her to look at some results. I waited for them to finish and asked if she had time after work to go for chai? She said she would text me.

I checked my phone every few minutes until she eventually messaged and asked me to meet her at 4 pm at the entrance if I was free. When we had met, she told me she started at seven every morning and told me how she loved going home early in time to help her mother cook or she helped her younger siblings with homework or coursework. I didn't recognise the feelings and the change in me; Tasneem made me feel happy. The day was much better when I saw her, even if we did not chat, but she waved and smiled from a distance. She was self-assured and determined, but I never saw her refuse help. I was touched by the way she treated Umayma, the other children and teenagers in her ward. She was the same with colleagues and other staff, polite to the auxiliary staff and generous with her smiles. She was sweet, patient and smart. I felt excited to have tea with her, though I rarely drank anything caffeinated in the late afternoon. Today would be an exception.

She beamed when she saw me, and I wondered how she felt about me. She was in her cycling clothes but still looked lovely. She looked thin and I wondered why, but she laughed and told me she always looked thinner in lycra than in her scrubs. She said a new cafe had opened and asked if we wanted to try it, but as always she said she didn't have much time. I nodded. I bought two chai lattes and wondered what kind of cake she liked. I chose two different ones, one with chocolate and another with almonds. Her eyes widened when I approached our table, and she scolded me for buying such delicious cakes when she was going home for her dinner, but then admitted all she had eaten that lunch time had been a packet of crisps and a pear a nurse had given her. I watched her eat; she was so delicate and enjoyed every mouthful, but she had divided both cakes in half and told me to eat mine, before she ate it. I told her I did not mind if she ate them both and I could buy more, but she laughed and wouldn't touch my share saying she didn't need any more cake. She watched me eat a few bites of cake and smiled. I offered to buy her something else, but she admitted she was now full and would eat later with her family. We chatted about the day, and I told her I had something to ask her and she looked at me with curiosity. I asked her if she would go on a date with me. She looked absolutely shocked, got up, gathered her things and then faced me and said that she was only that friendly with me because she thought I was gay, apologised and ran off. I was then more shocked and couldn't move for a while. I collected myself and ran after her, but when I got outside, I watched her cycle away on the busy road. I walked back to the hospital and drove home after cancelling my patients for the rest of that day. I felt gutted, sad and equally devastated. I couldn't work feeling like this. I would make up the missed appointments the next day. I was seething at my own stupidity, now I would lose my new friend, a friend I cared for so deeply.

I was surprised to see a WhatsApp invitation from Dr Tasneem later that evening. She always pretended to be angry when I called her Dr Tasneem and said I wasn't her patient, so I shouldn't be so formal, yet she never called me anything, but by my formal title and name. I accepted her WhatsApp invitation and went to change my clothes. I heard my mobile beep and found a long, apologetic message from her. She was really touched by what I had asked her, she apologised several times for assuming I was homosexual, told me she had nothing against gay men, but she would not have been so bold and friendly with me otherwise. She knew this was old-fashioned. She was so embarrassed. She said she would meet me and talk, but could I leave it for now.

I hated social media and rarely used it. I am not on any of the forums; I like telephoning people and speaking to them, even messaging frustrates and annoys me, except for the odd time when it is useful like sending an address or a quick message or email or, of course, now to find directions. I never liked having to update my Satnav or being led into a dead end. My sisters loved all that socialising on their phones and computers so I let them contact people, make arrangements and I waited to be told. I never wrote on any family chats, never accepted invitations, even for professional networks. I remember once an old pupil from school had found me at the hospital. He told me how hard it had been to find me on social media. Exactly! I did not want to be found. School had ended being bearable, but I had not kept in touch with a single pupil. I appreciated the usefulness of social media when contacting and staying in touch with family abroad. Social media was used by the most poor and illiterate as well as the wealthiest, but I hate how it distracted and stopped people talking directly. However, tonight I did not hesitate to accept Tasneem's invitation. I know I sound pathetic.

I didn't know whether to reply, but she would see I had read her message. I know how I felt when I didn't see her for a few days. I hated it when people did not reply to my calls when there was a serious issue that needed to be resolved. Twenty minutes had passed, so I sent her a message telling her that I understood, but I wanted to stress I was NOT gay and hoped that we could meet and sort everything in person. SOON.

I looked inside my fridge, but felt full after the cake. I had some soup and would heat it later if I felt hungry. I wondered whether to call Mum or my sisters, but I decided to leave it. They would interrogate me, and I was in no mood for that. I couldn't focus on work. I was never home this early and felt restless. I should have gone and finished my work. I felt guilty, so I sat and decided to watch TV and put on a movie. I made myself have some soup and checked my emails, did some admin work, showered and got ready for bed. I would read and hoped that would help me fall asleep.

Tasneem called me just as I got into bed. She told me that she was a nervous wreck. She couldn't wait until we met in person to talk to me so she had to call me instead, if only she knew how happy I felt to hear this, no matter what she said, I had not, at least, lost her. She kept apologising and I told her to stop. I asked her if she was seeing anyone and she said no. I asked her if she liked me, and she replied that she did, but she wasn't sure in what way. She saw us as good friends, close colleagues, liked seeing me in hospital and didn't want to spoil any of this. Oh, if she could see how happy all this made me feel, I had the biggest and silly smile on my face, but I stayed calm and soothed her instead. We talked for an hour until I heard her being called. She asked if I realised how late it was, her mum was telling her to go to sleep else she wouldn't be able to get up in the morning for prayers; she told me her mum forced her to do the dawn Fajr prayers every morning before she left for work, so she could be blessed for the rest of the day. She laughed and told me she didn't mind because it was such a short and quick prayer. She enjoyed this time with her mum and it helped her prepare for the day. I asked if she was already in bed and she said she was, so I told her to go to sleep in a commanding, but happy voice. We said good night and arranged to meet for lunch the next day. I fell asleep happily thinking of her in her bed.

I wasn't in the NHS hospital where Tasneem worked the next day, so I went in early to see my private clients, rearranged my afternoon appointments and rushed to the NHS hospital. She appeared as I was opening my door and then asked if I should be there or in my other job. I have never managed to lie, not even a white lie to her and one look at my face told her the truth. She laughed and we went in; she had brought food as she said she didn't want to talk about her private life in public. Some amazing smells were coming out of the bag of food, and I said I was hungry. I had forced some of the soup down last night, but had not enjoyed it at all. She said they were only leftovers, but we both knew that some food always tastes better the next day, especially when you are starving. She had found a microwave and everything was piping hot. I shut the door; I was particular about eating in my office; I did not like smells lingering in a space I used for consultation, business and meetings as I felt it was unprofessional, but since meeting Tasneem, everything about my life was changing. We ate slowly and talked.

Tasneem shared that she had never dated; she had gone out with a few of the men introduced to her, but always with a chaperone. She told me that her family, well her father, were really strict and whatever she did would impact on her younger sister and brother. She shared about a date with one man in her community. The first meeting had gone well and he said he was impressed she was a consultant. He asked if he could come to visit her at work. She wasn't sure, but they had been chatting for a few weeks and he asked so often; she finally agreed to meet him for coffee and would show him around her place of work. He had come and everything went fine. He bought her a coffee and then she showed him around. Tasneem told me that in her work, parents were always coming to thank her; there was a casual ease and comradery in her ward. Children would always want a hug, and of course, they had to be careful in how they dealt with them, but generally, there was openness and a lot of love. As Tasneem was walking with her potential suitor, some parents came and hugged Tasneem, and a few of her colleagues touched her on the arm and were very casual with her. The man with her said nothing, but Tasneem felt he became stiff and unfriendly. She said goodbye to him outside the hospital and the man hurried away. He blocked her later that day on his mobile phone and she didn't understand what was happening. A few women from their community rang Tasneem's mum later that day and said that the young man was describing Tasneem as being loose and like a prostitute because she hugged strangers and let people touch her. There are a few men, Muslim men especially, like this, but neither of us had directly encountered such closed minded and old-fashioned behaviour. After this, Tasneem had been very careful and wary in how she behaved in her courtship. I told her I hoped I would never ever behave like that. I am neither jealous nor do I have such primitive requirements of and from women.

Her father probably even now wouldn't approve of her dating, but she said she was keen and wanted to go out with me so that we could get to know each other better. I literally wanted to jump for joy and high five someone, but as always I maintained my calm and controlled exterior. She used the word keen and my heart was feeling overjoyed and skipped a beat. All this was ridiculous, why did I feel like this? I was not an emotional, easily excitable person, and I definitely wasn't a teenager. What I knew was that I had never felt like this before with anyone else. I liked the feeling even though it scared me a little bit. If things progressed, she said, then I would have to come to meet her family formally to do things properly, and I told her I did not mind. I was not so arrogant or lost from my traditions to appreciate that her family was more traditional. I understood that she did not want to lie and be secretive when she lived with them. She asked my age and we found I was five years older than her. I told her honestly that I never saw myself married, had never been in love, and like her, my family were always trying to pair me off with some woman, with a friend they knew or someone's daughter. We chatted and laughed for over two hours. I found her as before, honest, open and she had a manner that put me at ease. She jumped when she noticed the time on the clock on my wall; I walked her to her ward, and I had to return to my private patients. I was in no mood to work, and for some reason, I could not stop smiling. The world looked different, brighter and much happier.

She told her mother and her sister about me that night, but they decided not to tell her father just yet. I met her mum two weeks later when I dropped her home. I did not go in even though her mum insisted, but we chatted briefly at the door. I wanted to do everything by the proper process. When I told my parents, Mum was overjoyed, but not at all surprised. She told me she had often seen Tasneem, both in the hospital and at the home where Umayma was convalescing, and I asked her why she never mentioned it. Mum had told Popa and all my siblings about Tasneem, and they couldn't wait to meet her.

It was a week later when we kissed. I had taken her to see a play as she had always wanted to go to the theatre, and she had never afforded it before. She was successful, and I joked and asked her what she did with all her earnings. I really hoped that she would not turn out to be like Mimi, demanding, controlling and sucking me of all my dignity, always needing me to pay for everything and assuming that was my duty. I never minded as I knew I was wealthy, but I preferred to have some say in how the money I earned from my hard work was spent. Tasneem told me her story. She told me how her parents had come to the UK from East Africa due to political unrest in East Africa, and it had been a struggle ever since they arrived in London. Her father lost his menial job when she was sixteen as the factory, he worked in had gone into liquidation. Her father had no qualifications, and even though he was prepared to do any kind of work, he just could not find another job. Tasneem and her siblings had worked during every spare time they had, every weekend and summer holidays, giving their paltry salary to their parents. Her mum had worked in an Indian food factory, so they always had lots of food, but her dad had got depressed when he felt emasculated and her teenage years had been difficult.

Her dad now worked in a supermarket and her mum no longer worked as she had chronic back ache. Tasneem had bought the home they lived in because it had two downstairs sitting rooms, so one was converted and it allowed her parents to have a bedroom downstairs, as her mum found climbing stairs a challenge, even though she hadn't even turned fifty yet. Tasneem had been doing research to see if there was any available treatment, but at the moment, the best treatment, she told me, was acupuncture. I had laughed and Tasneem looked at me and I could see how concerned and worried she was about her mum, and I felt horrible. I had never believed in such alternative therapy and Tasneem, of course, soon changed my mind about this.

We had met earlier that day, had a light meal and Tasneem would not let me pay for anything else as the tickets were over a hundred pounds. She was so different from Mimi. We met for a walk Sunday afternoon; we never seemed to have any moments of dullness. We chatted or were happy smelling flowers and just walking, looking at the world around us. Tasneem felt stupid as she had not been able to see much of London, even though she was born here and spent all her life at home. She had never been able to go away to university; she got grants and funding, but she saved every penny to support her family. I told her not to worry as she had the whole of her life to sort that; I would be her guidebook to the world. We were both busy with commitments so we stole a moment to have a quick chai when I was in the NHS hospital, but I was finishing earlier these days, and we would try to fit in a cinema show or a brief meeting any chance we got. I had wished she didn't cycle as much as I liked dropping her home, but she liked her independence. I would drop her home after we went out and she did not like to have to take the bus when she left her bicycle at the hospital, but she did it as she knew I loved to drop her home and we had that extra fifteen minutes together.

The following weekend was a family gathering and Mum suggested I bring her, but we were both worried and Tasneem more than me. I did not want to make the same mistakes as I had done with Mimi, and Tasneem wanted us to be certain about us, then make a formal declaration to her father before we progressed to the next stage of our relationship. I told my parents this and they were surprised, but totally understood Tasneem's position. Tasneem did not want to offend and had called my mum to apologise and explain, but my mum stopped her and said that they totally understood and their love of her which was growing by the day had the additional factors of respect and care. We were both older, and I was sure we could get away without following every Muslim ritual and procedure, but for Tasneem, this was her first serious relationship, and she was cautious and careful. She did not want to hurt her father, did not want his disapproval or be accused of being devious. We were both happy and loved being together, but I saw periods of regret in Tasneem; I knew she felt guilty and sly. She never lied to her mother, but she knew her father suspected that life was changing for her and she had mentioned that she saw him look at her differently, almost asking her outright but too afraid to do so in case he would not like her response. She hated to make him feel like this.

She told me she had assumed that I had had many relationships, and I shared with her that I knew most people thought this of me and I never understood why. Tasneem laughed when I asked her why she had thought this of me. She mentioned my designer suits; I drove everywhere in a car that cost more than the deposit on their home. She described that she had found me aloof, slightly arrogant and a man of the world. I was a little upset by the judgments, but as always, she smiled, and I saw she was teasing me, though I wondered if there was any truth in what she said. I knew I kept myself to myself. I have never had many close or best friends, and despite what people think, I haven't been that interested in sleeping around with many different women. I saw Tasneem staring at me and she asked me about Mimi. I had told her I had one serious relationship, but I could not bring myself to tell her more. I wish I never had to tell her, but Tasneem knew something was terribly wrong, and she did not push me about Mimi at that time.

It had taken me over a year to get over Mimi; I wish I could have left the flat, and one of my sisters, Remi, asked me to move in with her, but the commute would have been long, difficult and terrible. I only drove a maximum of thirty minutes to work and then only when there was heavy traffic, and I found this hard enough. I had a car just to get from the three different locations I worked at quickly, but they were close and a fairly easy drive after all the hard work I did every day. I hated public transport, wasn't as brave as Tasneem to cycle, and I liked the convenience and independence that came with having my car. I knew it was a luxury and felt I deserved it with all my demanding work. I had been terrified of even smiling at a woman after Mimi and perhaps this explained my becoming even more reserved and buried in work. It was good to have time now to think, reflect and slowly recover.

I invited Tasneem out to dinner on Wednesday night. We had been dating only for a few months, but I had missed her when I didn't see her and wanted to have a proper evening with her rather than a quick break or a fleeting or stolen meeting. She asked if she could see my flat and she could cook, but I said I would get a take away as I knew she worked as hard as me, but she said she cooked with her mum most nights. Well, she would have a break from cooking, but the thought of taking her to a place I no longer liked distressed me. She saw me look worried and placed her hand on mine; it made me look at her and smile. No one except my mum, my popa and my sisters had this effect on me; she calmed and relaxed me. I was still worried; I hadn't managed to buy new furniture and just threw a throw over my beautiful, but paint splattered sofa. I had the walls painted and Mum had scrubbed my floors; she and my cleaner had scoured every section of the flat and got it as pristine as they could and managed to get rid of most stains. I wanted to throw away my Persian rugs, but Mum had removed some of the paint, and she insisted that what was left was bearable, didn't ruin the beauty of the rugs and I shouldn't worry about it, and so I kept the beautiful and very expensive rugs.

Tasneem wanted Mexican food; she loved to try new food and told me she rarely ate out. She had eaten popular commercial Mexican food like tacos and fajitas, but she hoped she could try something more authentic. Every time she cycled home, she passed and saw this elderly couple babysitting the children at a simple Mexican Cantina restaurant. She had stopped to say hello to the couple with the children, but the business had not been open when she cycled past so she had never tried their food. I had suggested an Indian restaurant assuming that she only ate halal, but she said she never worried about such things; it was her parents who were staunch about these things. She didn't want to telephone and order the food, but asked if we could stop outside that restaurant she had always wanted to eat at. I suggested eating there instead, but she reminded me she wanted to see my flat. There was no getting away from that. I relaxed and decided to savour the evening. I enjoyed watching her at the restaurant. She chatted to the man who told us it was his wife who did the cooking with her son and daughter-in-law. They lived above their small restaurant. I would never think to eat in such a place. Twenty minutes flew by, the man insisted we drink a juice he gave us for gratis and the wife had soon come to join in the chat. Tasneem got on with everyone; she was a marvel, always smiling and getting people to share their deep and intimate information within minutes of meeting. I just watched, nodded and listened. Tasneem had spent ages looking at the menu, but then asked the man what he recommended, telling him that the only food we didn't eat was any meat from a pig. She let the owner decide what we would eat that night. There were great smells coming out of the kitchen so I had no worries; Tasneem got out her purse to pay, but I reminded her that I had invited her so it was to be my treat. She let me pay without arguing, and I could see approval in the man's eyes when I did.

She said it would help her see my true self when she visited my home. I smiled nervously, and she told me to stop worrying. I rarely left work so early, and it was strange to see the children coming home from school and the roads were busier than I had ever experienced them; I usually left work no earlier than 7 pm, and it was often nearer 9 at night. I decided I must make more of an effort to get home when it is still light. It was good to see the hustle and bustle of daily life. The same place looked absolutely different at night, the road full of adults eating out and commuters rushing to their homes. I liked seeing teenagers gathering, laughing loudly and mothers with prams, tugging at older children to hurry along. Tasneem did the same as me; she watched intently, and

I could see she was lost in her thoughts. I parked and she collected the food and her rucksack. I hadn't noticed earlier that she had dressed specially for me after changing from her normal scrubs; I told her how beautiful she looked and saw her blush.

We took the private lift to the flat, said hello to the concierge, who was surprised to see me so early, and I introduced Tasneem to him as I hoped that he would see her many more times at my home. He gave me a parcel and some letters and had already called the lift ready for us to go up to my flat. I let Tasneem go into the lift first, and she said how that surprised her as these days with equality, she never knew how to manage men holding doors and letting her walk ahead. I said she had to do what was comfortable, but this was how I was taught to behave, and I think with us, Tasneem liked my manners and politeness. At least I was constantly amusing her with it. The number of times we had hit our heads, she was always wanting to please, and I always wanted to be helpful, so we both went for it and banged our foreheads.

She actually gasped when she entered the flat and cooed at everything; she had been surprised by the private underground parking; she was stunned by the lifts and the flat was, she said, nothing like she had seen. She described it as stunning and luxurious. She told me she was glad I hadn't visited her home. It was an ex-council house; they were lucky to have such a large home with a garden in London, but it was dowdy compared to my modern, minimalist, airy and light flat. I have never thought about such things; my family was wealthy and my grandfather had left all us children a hefty lump sum, such that I had bought this flat when I was still a student doctor having paid a large part of what it cost with my inheritance. My father had also helped even though I had not wanted him to, and he told all of us he would rather see the joy from his money when he was alive than wait to die and leave us money that he would never know how it had been spent. As I earned so well, my mortgage was now already paid off. My parents joked how this was their city flat, and they knew they were always welcome to visit and stay. In fact, I loved it when they did.

Tasneem threw her shoes off as soon as she entered; she then suggested we eat whilst the food was warm. I showed her the kitchen and dining table, and she took out the food parcels whilst I got plates, cutlery, glasses and a jug of water. I placed some serviettes. Tasneem was always starving; she was terrible at eating during the day, often failed to take her lunch break, but she never worked beyond four unless of course there was an emergency. We had chicken Tamales starters, which were stunningly delicious, wrapped in banana leaves, and they were piping hot, and I could have eaten more than two. Then I saw the refried beans; there was steak cooked in chilli, roasted corn on the cob and a vegetable medley. We talked about childhood whilst we ate; our lives were vastly different, and I found Tasneem's stories fascinating and vivid. She had always been happy, and like me, her family were the central key element of her life. She was fearful of her very disciplined father, but loved him and adored her mum and siblings. Her mum's mother had lived with them for eleven years when her mum's father, Nanna, had passed away. Tasneem told me how she had come to her graduation, loudly telling everyone that was her granddaughter! She had shared Tasneem's bedroom, brought her hot milk with powdered almonds and cardamoms to help her memorise for her exams.

She was always cooking and cleaning; she taught her to make sweets and snacks, even though they told her how easy it was to just buy them in Tooting, but she insisted nothing made outside ever tasted as good as homemade food. Tasneem still missed her nannima; she had two of her sarees and had never worn them, but she loved looking at them from time to time. Tasneem had kept all her religious knickknacks in her bedroom to this day; she found it comforting and made it seem like her nannima had never left.

Tasneem loaded the dishwasher whilst I changed from my suit into jeans and a shirt. I couldn't believe we had managed to eat all the food. I came back to find everything had been cleaned, put away and she was standing staring. I wanted her to always feel at home when she was with me, but she was polite and unassuming. I asked her if she wanted some chai, and she shook her head to indicate no. I suggested we sit down. We were too full for a dessert and a hot drink; I only had some chocolate and fruit, but Tasneem shook her head, saying she could manage nothing more to eat. She asked about the stains on the stunning rugs, and I sat her down on my sofa. I wanted to put some music on, but she said she liked the quiet. She had to go soon and so wanted this peaceful time with me.

I told her about Mimi. She didn't say a single word and when I stopped talking, I was thinking that this is the end of us, but Tasneem leaned into me and kissed me. It wasn't passionate; she was gentle, loving and sweet. I kissed her back frantically, and she placed her hand on my cheek and looked up at me. I kissed her some more but more gently. I wanted to gather her in my arms and take her into the bedroom and make love to her, but I resisted. She looked at the time and said she had to call her mum, and I listened to her speak lovingly to her mum in her mother tongue of Gujarati. I asked if I should take her home and she said she had told her mum she would be late. She sat next to me, turned to look at me and sat quietly whilst she held my hand.

We chatted for another hour; we sat and held hands, and I wanted to kiss her again, but she asked so many questions about Mimi and what had happened. I felt ashamed, and she told me not to be and kissed me on my cheeks and then my lips. She just wanted to know and hoped that she wouldn't have to ask about her after tonight. I asked her if it hadn't put her off me, and she shook her head. She had the same look she used when she was with her young child patients; she was caring, considerate and interested in all I had to say. She interjected and asked questions that made me think about issues with Mimi I had ignored and put up with. There was no judgement; I saw flushes of anger on her face but a lot of sympathy and love. She couldn't believe how easily I had allowed her to control and dominate, and she made me promise that I would never let her treat me like that. Tasneem knew she was strong, assertive, sometimes stubborn and hoped she would never control and bully anyone.

I wished she could stay, but she told me she had to go home now as she was struggling to stay awake. She went to the bathroom and I put on my jacket. I watched her gather her things and put her shoes on. She fitted perfectly in the flat, but she never stayed here. She visited often; we kissed, but she asked if I minded if we waited to make love. She told me she had never been with a man. I knew she wanted to wait until we married or were at least engaged, and I wasn't sure if I would be able to wait, but I would never force the issue, and

I certainly would never force her to do anything she was not ready to do. She was shy when I even touched her arm; at work, she blushed if I kissed her in greeting lightly on her lips, and I asked her if she wanted me to stop and she said she didn't, but it was taking her time to get used to the situation. I felt exhilarated and content. She told me all the time that she felt like a sixteen-year-old, ecstatically happy, silly and clumsy. Mum told me that the name 'Tasneem' means 'the Fountain of Paradise' and I had indeed found my Elysium. My mum refers to Tasneem as my Jannah, the Muslim word for heaven or paradise. Mum had always called her Jaan, the life and soul of the children she treated. We would all discover that she was more than this; she would turn out to be my elixir and one that would save my life.

Chapter 3
Coma

I could hear Tasneem's father, he was gentle and very upset as he talked to me. I was surprised at his reaction as when I went to formally visit him that first time, he had been very stern, raised his voice, kept shaking his head and was quite scary. Tasneem asked me to bring my parents, to dress up and come with presents at our first formal meeting with her parents when she finally let me ask their permission to date and marry her. I was annoyed when she told me about the presents. She always praised me for my manners, but she told me she didn't mean flowers and chocolates; she told me what her parents or tradition would consider appropriate. Mum called Tasneem and told her not to worry; she knew exactly what was necessary in our Muslim traditions; they spoke to each other all the time. After about seven months of dating, Tasneem asked me if I was serious about her, and I was hurt that she could ask me such a thing. She made me feel an extreme of emotions; I was overjoyed and easily offended by her. One thing was clear, I, myself, never wanted to hurt her or ever let her down. She made me happy, extremely content and beyond what I had expected 'love' to be or feel like.

She started to come to my family lunches; we stayed a weekend at Mum's, and unlike Mimi, she was not offended that Mum had put us in separate bedrooms. My sisters loved

Tasneem the minute they met her and she loved them in return. If they knew we were visiting my parents, they either popped in or came to stay. Mum and my sisters took Tasneem shopping to select gifts for her family as we didn't want to take anything that was inappropriate or not to their taste. Tasneem said she wanted to pay, and Mum pretended to be offended. My parents realised that there was a chasm of difference in class between the two families, but Mum was a compassionate and generous person, as was Tasneem. Tasneem was already more of a daughter to my parents than an outsider. I had selected a diamond and ruby ring as these were her birthstones, a matching necklace, earrings and two white gold bracelets with matching gemstones to her ring as an engagement present and was desperate to give them to her. I told Mum not to tell Tasneem about these. This was to be my surprise engagement present to her if her father agreed and gave us permission to marry.

It hadn't gone well. We visited as planned one Sunday afternoon. Tasneem's mum had cooked a feast of snacks, but her father appeared uncomfortable and a little angry. When my father brought up my wanting to marry his daughter, he had shaken his head and looked upset and filled with fury. He said we were two disparate and the families did not know each other; we were not the same culture; he was happy I was Muslim, but we were just too different and incompatible. He had stunned us all, but my parents remained calm; they did not storm out, be rude or take offence, but asked his permission to let us at least see how it went. He did not want to accept our presents, but Mum in her serene manner gave them to him and said it would be our honour if he would accept. With the help of Tasneem's mum, they cajoled and debated with Tasneem's father. We ate; I felt sick, but tried to peck at the food Tasneem had placed on my plate and her eyes willed me to eat. I drank my chai, and she poured more into my cup; it had ginger and cardamom, and I started to feel better and relaxed. Eventually, Tasneem's mum took the presents, and she hugged my mum. Her father was not happy, but he gave permission for us to meet and for the families to get to know each other. Tasneem's siblings came into the room and shook my hands, her young sister Tara gave me a tight hug, and I saw her father watching. We stayed about two hours and left with a promise that they would come to visit my parent's home in two weeks' time. I had seen Mum place the jewellery in her handbag; it was too soon to formally have an engagement, and instead, my parents came to stay a few days with me as they could see I was upset. They thought that it would be better to host the engagement at their home, and I could give the jewellery to Tasneem then.

My sisters had organised a conference call so that we could all talk together, and they called a few minutes after we got home to hear every detail of the engagement and were a little sad when Mum told them it hadn't happened. They did not lose hope; they trusted that Tasneem would sort it out. Tasneem had seen my face, knew I was worried and she called me later, feeling as sad as me. She wondered if my parents were changing their mind and asked bluntly if I felt the same. It was my turn to tease and help her relax. I told her I loved her. I had never said it to her before and I amazed myself why it had taken me so long. I really loved her. Deeply. The words of every love song I had ever heard but never taken seriously rushed through my mind. This was how I felt, every word reflected and voiced aloud my feelings and thoughts. She did not hesitate in telling me she loved me more. My mum heard me talking to Tasneem and asked to speak to her and took the phone from my hand. She also reassured Tasneem, easily telling her how much the family loved and wanted her as part of the family. She was not to worry and everything would sort itself out. She asked Tasneem to visit them whilst they were in London, and Tasneem said she would come on Tuesday evening.

It was as if I was looking at myself from somewhere high above; I didn't recognise this thin man, bandaged and attached to a range of different machines that were keeping him alive. I was always screaming out words, but then I saw I had been intubated, how was I managing to scream and talk? I realised it was not real. I questioned why my father-in-law was in my room. I saw he was holding my hand; he was reading from the Quran and had blessed the water and placed a few drops on my lips. Where was Tasneem and my family? He wet his clean handkerchief and wiped my forehead, placed his head on my chest and was crying as he read various sections of the Quran. This man hadn't approved of me dating, never mind marrying his gorgeous daughter, so why was he here and crying? I felt utter confusion but shared his sadness. Inside, I was crying profusely.

They, Tasneem's family, had arrived thirty minutes early, but Popa was so happy and not at all thrown off by this or offended. He knew and understood it was due to nerves and believing that we were above them and they had to be subservient to us. My parents soon dismissed this. Popa took hold of Tasneem's father by putting his arm around his shoulder, called him brother, bhai Sefuddin and welcomed him warmly to their home. Tasneem's mum had bought some plants and sweets, and she tried to follow Mum into the kitchen, but my younger sister, Gulshan, shooed both mums into the garden. It was a beautiful day so we had planned a barbeque in the garden. We first had cold drinks, coffee, chai and snacks, then Mum showed Tasneem's family around their beautiful house. Tasneem had visited a few times, her mum knew but not her father and so she dutifully followed. Then the men sat and watched the women walk around the garden talking about plants and smelling the flowers. My older sister, Remi, came with her husband and two children; they ran to Tasneem, then to her parents and formally greeted them with "As salamu alaikum, Uncle ji and Aunty!" They threw themselves at everyone with hugs, letting their heads be patted and cheeks be kissed. They were miniatures of my siblings and me, though I was not nearly as confident as them even as an ageing adult. They loved Tasneem who always snuck sweets out of her bag for them. Today, it was Tasneem's mum who did this, and I smiled at how we turned into our parents.

Tasneem's father relaxed more and more. The families were informal, but an abundance of respect was shown to him and his family. The males in the family debated how best to barbeque the meats; we all knew it was the women who did most of the work in preparing, making salads and desserts. We set the tables and a picnic for the children on a spread on the lawn. Tasneem and I sat with our parents and her siblings whilst mine waited on us and served the food, making sure the children finished their food. I really believe that of all my family, I might be the biggest snob, the others are very easy-going and have a lovely mix of my mum's Iranian heritage and my popa's Indian/ Pakistani heritage. They showed no airs and graces, were hospitable, gracious and polite.

Tasneem's siblings had joined in to help my siblings without being asked or prompted and refused to sit and be served. They fitted in, chatted and were not at all shy. They too became part of our extended family, and I could see both sets of parents happy at the developments over the day; there was no ceremony and formality, though everyone gave Tasneem's father the regard that was due to him and deserved as he was starting to let go of his eldest daughter.

My popa's family had fled India during partition in 1947 to Iraq instead of to Pakistan, as they had heard of terrible massacres of Muslims happening, and then moved to England. My grandfather was a canny businessman who had invested all their wealth into gold that our grandmother had hidden by sewing into the lining of her clothes. When they arrived in London, my grandfather had sold the gold and bought property, two homes in Chelsea and one on the river bank in Battersea as well as their own home. He sold these for millions of pounds in profit some years later, reinvested some of the money and he had used the remaining money to educate all his children in private school such that my father, his brother and sister were now hugely successful and rich, as were we and all our cousins. My grandfather helped each of his children buy their own home, and he had continued to do this with his grandchildren.

Mum went to check on the food and arrangements for lunch; she did not bring out the cutlery, just spoons and we all ate with our hands as we watched Tasneem's father do this, and we did not want to make him feel awkward. The meat on the barbeque was already smelling wonderful; the children sat with roasted corn on the cob in their hands and faces covered in melting butter. Gulshan and Tara were trying to roast stuffed peppers. The children were happy; they loved eating with their hands, and it was an effort to make the youngest sit still long enough to eat; they loved running around, a chicken drumstick in their hand and face covered in sauce.

Tasneem's father was chatting to me remembering the barbeque during his first visit to meet my parents. Could he see me smiling when he talked about how he had loved to see the children running around and longed to be a grandfather. He had got up to make a speech, and I saw all of Tasneem's family looking shocked and fearful of what he might say. He called Tasneem over to him. Tasneem had dressed traditionally for the first time; when we visited, she wore a lovely long top over her trousers, but today, she had a long blue skirt with an embroidered top and a matching scarf draped over her head. She had borrowed some of her mum's jewellery and wore matching shoes, which frustrated her as the heels kept sinking into the lawn. She had made me promise her not to wear a suit, as if I would do so at my parent's homely gathering, and I was in casual formal clothes of beige chinos, a white shirt and one of my grandfather's colourful traditional waistcoats that my sisters had tried to steal any chance they got. I missed wearing the cufflinks that Mimi had taken. Saiffuddin called me and I got up; he held Tasneem's hand and said how proud he was of her, how much she had helped her family, but the time had come to now pass her to her future husband. Everyone clapped and cheered; the children got up and ran around the standing adults, not really understanding what was happening but aware that everyone was happy. There were tears, laughter and lots of hugs. One of my older nephews put on some cheerful Hindi music, and Tasneem told me it was about a couple getting engaged and the joy around it. Gulshan and her husband got up, danced and clapped their hands, pulling Tasneem and I to dance with them.

Mum had gone and came back with the jewellery; she asked for the music to be turned down and made everyone sit down. Popa stood at her side, but he let her speak. She passed me the jewellery box and I got on my knees and asked Tasneem to marry me; she was crying so much she didn't reply and her mum got up and said, "Yes, yes, Tasneem, please say YES!"

Tasneem's father cried as he spoke to me in this hospital bed. He kept saying sorry and how all he was doing was his fatherly duties. I had never judged him ill; I knew Tasneem loved him, and we grew close over the years. He and Popa got on very well. He had loved the formal engagement organised at my parent's home; he had quickly changed his mind about my family. He whispered that he had still been unsure about me, but he knew that Tasneem would fit easily and well into my family and that was all a father could want. Now he loved me and was as proud of his daughter and son-in-law, as any parent would be of such wonderful children. He told me how much he loved my children and was now a proud grandfather, a nanna.

I heard Tasneem return to my hospital room; she had brought chai and snacks for her father, and he told her how he had been talking to me about the barbeque. I could smell the chai and was desperate to have a large mugful of it. They continued to chat as if I was talking as well. I knew Tasneem would know that I could hear. She knew. At the engagement barbeque at my parents' home, we ate, danced, ate some more and chatted until the evening, and when they got ready to leave, my family insisted they stay longer. Chai was made, there was ice cream and pastry, and after that even Tasneem's mum was ready to leave. Tasneem stayed and her brother drove her parents and the family home. Mum told them that I would drop Tasneem to their home on Sunday night. Tasneem still wore her engagement ring; she had made me make it bigger each time she was pregnant and when it hurt her finger, and I had to have it made smaller when she had lost the baby weight. I wanted to get it re-made, but she threatened to divorce me if I did that.

Her father held her hand and was playing with her ring. He got up to leave; our children were staying with them in their home and he left saying he wanted to see them before they went to sleep. The hospital didn't like us bringing my sons to see me; they said it would scar them for life, but we never shielded them from the truth. Tasneem just said, "Imagine the regret if they never saw their father again; it is their right and my choice whether my children see their father." The hospital could not dispute this and kept saying that they were not in agreement. She brought my children to me most weekends and occasionally after school when they begged her they needed to see me. I also needed to see them! Tasneem's father asked if she was coming home, and when Tasneem shook her head, he said they would return with the boys early the next day so we could read to them and they could see their father.

I was struggling to remember why I was in a coma. What had happened? Was there a car accident, no, I didn't think so, as I was a fairly decent driver, but why couldn't I remember? I know that the police came a few times to ask if I was recovering; I heard them whisper to each other that I was gone, dead and they wouldn't be able to identify my killer. I screamed, "What killer, who tried to kill me?" I heard Tasneem scold them for talking like that in front of me; she took them out, and I could hear her voice raised, even with the door closed, but I couldn't make out exactly what she was saying to them.

Tasneem talked to me and asked if I remembered our trip to India. We decided on a spring wedding. I wanted to marry her as soon after the engagement barbeque as possible, but she was the eldest in her family, the first to get married and I was the only son in my family, so both parents wanted a big wedding. I did not want this at all, but I had no say in the matter, both families were united in what they all wanted. The compromise was a spring wedding, but we were all first going to go to India for a visit, a holiday, shopping and to get everything needed for the wedding. I refused to go saying that it was the women who needed to shop and I knew nothing about such things, but again, I was out-voted. We left on the 10th of December and returned on the 3rd of January. I had been dreading this trip, but it turned out to be fantastic. It was my father's treat. He paid for everyone and he, together with Tasneem's father, planned in detail what we would be doing, seeing and visiting each and every day. We started with a visit to both their parents' homes, then we went to Delhi and did all the touristic trips ending in a visit to the Taj Mahal. It was stunning, and it was more than what any of us imagined. This stunning mausoleum of white marble which is dedicated to love, serenity and with its commitment to intimacy and family. Tasneem told me that we would return one day and do the same trips when our children were older and would appreciate the sites, its history and beauty.

I was then forced to fly to Mumbai with the women to shop for clothes, everything and anything needed for our wedding, whilst our fathers stayed in the north of India exploring and meeting other family and friends from years gone. We were fitted into ornate clothes, bought material and we had hired a Durgi or tailor who with his efficient team of employees were constantly busy sewing every outfit we bought, clothes for the whole family, presents for my sisters, their husbands and the children, for relatives and outfits for the various ceremonies. I watched the women, they were in their element, happy and chattering. My mum had wanted to do this for her daughters, but both had had smaller weddings in local hotels after shopping in Wembley in London for their one wedding outfit. Mum had wanted one of her children to get married in Iran, but none of us were willing, so now she threw herself in my wedding arrangements. Tasneem's mum and Tasneem had so much fun. I spent a lot of time watching them, drinking sweet spicy chai or fresh fruit juice or from green coconuts with holes burrowed and straws sticking out of them.

My family let Tasneem's family select the Asian wedding venue, and we were in trepidation, but it was a gorgeous location and venue, a specialised Indian wedding banqueting hall. It was tasteful and easily fit the six hundred guests invited. I was appalled when the numbers rose, but we decided to leave no one out, this was the last wedding in my family for my generation and the first in Tasneem's family. We invited every family, friend, colleagues from work and community members; there were so many different cultures, religions and ages from babies to the elders. Family and friends came from various parts of the UK and some from abroad. We had childhood friends, and I was so happy to invite Tim, Simon, Puleen and Gita, though only Tim and Gita could come with their own families as Simon and Puleen had returned to Africa years ago.

The actual wedding or Nikaah was small and intimate and held at the mosque. We just invited immediate family and very close friends, even then there were just over a hundred guests. Tim was one of my best men with Rahim, but Tasneem had four of her closest friends as her sai or bridesmaids. Tasneem's family insisted on paying for this part of the wedding and my parents did not argue. We both wore traditional Muslim clothes, the type of clothing I never wore, even when I was a child. I was westernised to my core and rebelled when Mum had tried to dress me in traditional clothes when I reached teenage years. Tasneem chose a pale lime colour, which was very unusual; she refused to wear the green and red wedding colours. She looked stunning, her hands and feet were covered in intricate mehndi or henna patterns; she wore the gold my parents gave her as Tasneem refused to accept the wedding trousseau Mum had wanted to buy, though she had relented and let us buy her wedding clothes and jewellery which was traditionally our right. She knew how much the trip to India had cost and never took advantage of our wealth. Her father insisted on paying for some of the accommodation, and Tasneem bought all her other clothes; she paid for the presents and even my Nikaah clothes as in her traditions, the bride bought the groom clothes for the Nikaah.

That wedding or shadhi night we stayed in the Dorchester Hotel, both families' children had decorated the hotel room with roses; petals were strewn and there were some presents for us. The Nikaah was just after Jummah prayers. I was at the mosque and prayed for the first time in years. I was already dressed in my Nikaah clothes, and after the prayers, Tasneem's sister Tara came and tied fresh roses around my head such that they dangled down like a veil from my gold wedding hat. I heard a commotion and was told that Tasneem had arrived, but I would not see her yet. She sat behind the curtain with her bridesmaids, sisters, my sisters and our mums. The other women invited sat behind them. I heard the click of the cameras and a video was taken of her and of me. I sat opposite Tasneem's father and the priest was to our side, a string was tied around our hands and one end was sent to Tasneem for her to hold. The Nikaah is actually a marriage contract between the groom and the bride's father. It involves the tying together of two families, hence the string being used to symbolise tying and binding people together. Prayers were said and then we took turns to reply, 'Nam', which meant we agreed with the vows being read. At the end, Tasneem was asked one final time if she agreed to marry me and the Nikaah ended when she agreed she did.

I got up, greeted her father with a salam or a kiss to his right hand; he gave me a hug to my surprise, and then I went to all the males to greet each one in turn. My family and eventually I was brought to meet Tasneem who in turn did salam and kissed my close family. She was told to demand money from me before she undid my veil; we both knew I would give her whatever she wished, but we had to pretend to disagree and play the games demanded by tradition, and we were finally allowed to greet each other. How I wished I could kiss her, but that is not allowed or considered appropriate. We sat down on a kind of throne that had been arranged for us, our hands and fingers would often touch as family and friends came to wish us well; we were given sweets, money and presents even though we had insisted on no one bringing or giving us anything. Envelopes of money were given to us such that the contents exceeded the cost of the wedding so I insisted Tasneem's family get to keep all of the monetary presents. A late lunch was served in the hall next door to the main mosque. I don't remember what we ate, but Tasneem remembered every detail. There were various savoury snacks, Indian sweets, followed by biryani opulent with saffron and cashew nuts followed by kulfi cones as it was a lovely warm day. We also had two albums of photos that documented it all and which my children never tired of looking at.

It was rare that Tasneem was alone in my hospital room. Either hers or my mum, sisters, brother and other extended family took turns to sit with her. Occasionally, friends and colleagues would drop in with a drink for Tasneem, hug her and pat my hand. However, at night she made them all go home and said she needed to be alone with me. It was during these times that she whispered stories and shared our intimate moments from the past eight years spent married to me. It was like she was forcing me to remember, to get better and wake up. If only she knew that it was all working. She would lay her head next to mine or on top of my chest; sometimes she would sneak into my bed and I worried she would plunge into deep sleep and fall off the bed.

She talked about our first night together. I was desperate to have her in my arms so I could make love to her. We had often lay close before we were married, but she did not want me to touch her intimately and I had always respected her wishes. We both knew that had I started, I might not have been able to stop. She told me she had waited so long, had almost given up hope of finding the right man and of getting married. Surely, we could wait a little while longer? At almost thirty years, she was considered a spinster, and she worried about the gossip and its impact on her family. Her sister, Tara, had been dating for two years and was desperate to marry. Tasneem had told her to do it, but she had refused. Her wedding was in a month's time. Tasneem had asked if she and Tara could marry together and I said I did not mind, but her sister would not agree. She worked in a doctor's surgery, and she did not want to steal Tasneem's day. We tried to explain that it was wrong for her to think like that, but she refused to change her mind saying that we were trying to stop her having her rights to annoy me as much as possible during the various wedding ceremonies as was the right of my new sister-in-law! We had given in to her.

It was early when everyone left us in our hotel room after the Nikaah, and I couldn't believe we were finally married. My best man, my older sister, Remi's husband, promised to collect us at eleven the next morning so that we could go home to get ready for the wedding reception to be held on the next day, which was Saturday. Tasneem asked if I would be upset if she had a bath. Normally, the man was supposed to undress his bride; there were all these rituals and traditions, but she said she was hot. I wasn't sure what to say; I felt hot in my wedding clothes, wanted her so desperately but would never rush this nor do anything that she did not want. Tasneem then turned around and said she hoped I would help her to take off her outfit which would be very difficult if she had to do it by herself. I grabbed her gently and kissed her, and she started to undo the many tiny buttons on my jacket and shirt. She had to tell me how to take off the pins that held the scarf around her hair, which was arranged beautifully. I lifted her hair up, kissed her neck, her chin and those delicious lips. There were so many safety pins holding her scarf in place around her bodice and on the back of her skirt. I even found a few safety pins in her hair used to hold the scarf in place. I took off the garlands of flowers. Next I undid her jewellery; she wore the set my family gave her, and she showed me what she had borrowed from her mum. She had a gold chain draped around her hair, held with many hairpins and this came off. We placed all the jewellery carefully in a bag so as not to forget any of the precious objects in the room hidden in bedding or under any of the covers. I started to undo the buttons on her blouse and discovered the lace underwear that matched her wedding outfit. I kissed the top of her breasts and struggled to undo her skirt. She showed me how it did up, undid it and let it slip to the floor. She picked up her clothes and hung them on the chairs; they were too precious to leave crumpled on the floor. I had never seen her in her underwear. Tasneem was normally very shy, but she removed my jacket and shirt and pulled me into the bathroom.

We were in the bridal suite, and it was made for romance. There were flowers in the bathroom, a range of bubble bath oils and a jacuzzi that made the bubbles float up to the ceiling. We filled the bath and put in as much bubble bath as we could. We giggled and spent ages inside the warm and fragrant waters, we both kissed every part of each other's body. Tasneem and I were shy, but we got lost in our play and romance. The slightest touch made me shiver and she made the sweetest sounds as I kissed her. I have never forgotten that night, the touch and how I felt. As she breathed next to my face in the hospital, I felt the same emotions of that first night we made love as I lay in the sterile hospital bed. I wanted to put my arms around her, why would they not move?

I wrapped her in a towel and carried her to the bed. Tasneem was mumbling in her sleep, and she had done the same that night. She placed her arms around my neck and told me she trusted me a thousand per cent. The toiletries made her smell perfumed and her skin was as soft as candy floss. Candy floss, why was I thinking of candy floss? It was linked to a childhood memory, but it wouldn't come to me. Tasneem had been talking about our wedding and so I was recalling everything she had whispered in my ears before she drifted off to sleep. Making love to a virgin is hard; I did not want to hurt her at all, and our playfulness in the bath had her aroused. We couldn't stop kissing each other; she said she didn't really know what she was doing even though she had tried to read everything she could on what was to happen during sex. I told her not to worry, she was doing fine and there was no need to hurry. We did not rush; we kissed and chatted. Making love to Tasneem felt natural, relaxed and it made her very ticklish, giggly, and we laughed a lot throughout the evening and night.

It was still early and she was starving; I had finally seen her naked, yet she was still shy and pulled a bathrobe and wrapped herself in one that was far too big for her. She went into the bathroom and washed; Muslims always do this after being intimate. There was a basket of fruit, cakes, biscuits and chocolate. She came back and made some tea for both of us and brought much of the food and placed it on our bed. I got up; I was not shy and walked naked to the bathroom but returned with a towel wrapped around my middle after I had washed as I knew this would make her more comfortable and less shy. I came and sat behind her, wrapped my arms around her; she turned her head, and as I went to kiss her she popped a piece of mango into my mouth and smiled. She turned around and kissed me. We feasted and checked the television, but neither of us were concentrating on what was on; we distracted each other with a touch or another kiss. I turned the TV off and undid her bathrobe.

When I woke up, Tasneem was curled up in the chairs she always put together so she could lie across them to stretch her legs out. She always kept a sleeping bag in my room. I wanted her next to me in our bed. I hated this, seeing her in a sleeping bag, rather than lying next to me. I couldn't remember how much time had passed. I couldn't stop the tears; I was crying yet no sound came out and my eyes wouldn't open. I tried and tried. Tasneem got up, stretched and kissed me; she always placed some water on my lips after washing my face with a cloth. I could see her, yet I think my eyes were shut. I could definitely smell her, sometimes she wore attar and other times I was surprised to smell her with one of the perfumes I had bought for her many years ago. That confusion, I felt so afraid that I would never wake up. I needed her and she felt this as she sat next to me and held my hand, telling me everything would be fine very soon. She left me to go to the bathroom, and I wanted to scream and tell her not to let go of my hand. I knew she would be back soon, but anytime she was not close to me made me afraid.

We slept better than we expected. I had wanted to make love to her again and again, but instead, we had both fallen asleep as even sitting whilst getting married was more tiring than we anticipated. We had another busy but fun day to come and woke up excited. We got up and bathed, then performed the special prayers. As she went to dress, I called and ordered breakfast. They were very quick in bringing us a feast; we had a balcony that faced Hyde Park, so we sat and ate and ate and ate. Tasneem looked at me and felt shy again; I told her to stop it, but even my laughter did not help her. I started to worry and when she saw what she called 'that look', she came and placed her arms around me. We finished almost all the food, croissants, fruit, muesli, poached eggs and toast. We had freshly squeezed orange juice, tea and coffee, which tasted delicious with all the delectable food I had ordered.

Our families came earlier than we expected, but thankfully, we were decent and dressed. There were three car loads of people, and they performed more rituals. Tasneem's sister Tara was supposed to cover her hair in coconut oil and massage her head, but Tasneem had already washed her hair and she did not want to wash it again for the reception, so she made Tara put only a tiny bit of oil in her hair but made Tara give her the full treatment otherwise. There was a massage and Tasneem kept saying MORE, to our pretend protestations of we were ready to leave and carry on with the celebrations. Gulshan rubbed her back, massaged her neck and I heard them whispering, asking questions about the night and there was a lot of giggling. We were ready and packed, so I stood on the balcony with all the men. They helped themselves to the food that had not been eaten, more drinks and pastries were ordered, and we left after an hour and a half. It is usual for the bride to go to the groom's home, but my parents' home was too far to drive to and return for the reception, so as my parents had stayed at my older sister Remi's home, we went there to get ready. I had a huge surprise for Tasneem, but I was too nervous to tell her about it just yet. I had decided, instead, to show her after the wedding reception.

Our reception was planned as a mixture of Iranian, Indian and British culture and traditions. I wore a suit as did most of the younger men, but the women, the older people and children all dressed in traditional clothes. Today, Tim would also act as a best man. All our white friends had made an effort to buy or borrow Asian clothes and looked fabulous. Normally, the couple who is central to the marriage arrives late and there is chaos, but Tasneem and I did not want that. We were ready and arrived on time, possibly a little too early. People came and said hello or found a table to sit at. It was an enormous venue, but I think we managed to greet everyone throughout the day. We arrived together and as we were going to sit in an area that was slightly raised, Tasneem's brother came and told me to take my shoes off before I sat down. Much to my dismay, before any of my best men could save my shoes, they were taken and a ransom was demanded for their return. The evening was full of such pranks. We settled in our seats, Tasneem wore a two-piece cream Indian dress; it was clearly Asian covered in fine embroidery and tiny beads but not dissimilar to a wedding dress. This was paid for by my parents and Tasneem actually chose it with my mum and let her pay for it without any argument. She covered her head with a matching chiffon scarf that trialled behind her. She wore heels and was only a few centimetres shorter than me. I normally towered over her. I had gotten ready in about fifteen minutes and I now understood why it had taken her over an hour. Her make-up was subtle but flawless; her hair was intricately woven around her head scarf, her nails were painted, and she beamed to everyone. Some brides play at being coy, but no one doubted our joy that day when they met the two of us.

Drinks and starters were served. Alcohol is forbidden in Islam, and we decided to respect our elders as none of them drank. We could have had a bar, but Tasneem's parents were very strict about that so my parents were happy to oblige. Some of my family drank but never at home and none of us minded that there was no alcohol. I know some of our friends found that strange as both Tasneem and I went to the pub with them, though Tasneem had never drunk alcohol. She told me she had tried everything. Had vomited after a shot of tequila and that had put her off drinking forever. There were so many different juices, fizzy drinks and mocktails, it didn't matter. The food was incredible, all home cooked by friends of Tasneem's parents. The buffet had not yet been set up, but when it was, it was efficient and never ran out of food.

Soon the wedding ceremonies began, and there were two small screens set up so everyone could see what was happening. Tasneem and I joked that we felt like celebrities on stage. Tasneem's mum performed some rituals with coconut – a symbol of purity and fertility; we had different women and girls blessing us by circling our heads with the decorated coconut, a small sweet was placed in our mouth so that our life would be forever sweet, more envelopes of money were slipped into our hands and then my mum was invited to come and bless us in the same way. Both fathers gave short speeches, my two best men made speeches and had everyone laughing at my expense. As the waiters started to set up the buffet, there was singing and some Indian dancing. My wonderful cousins and their children had prepared a wonderful, choreographed dance, which they performed without any shyness. There was clapping, whistling and joyful jeering demanding more or encouraging those dancing on the floor.

The buffet was laid out and people started their early dinner, people came to say hello to us and I had wanted to go to visit each table, but we never managed to get up and leave as a stream of people came to greet us. Our food was brought to us and despite the huge breakfast, we hadn't eaten lunch so we were enticed by the wonderful smells and were ready for some food. Family and friends came and each wanted to bless us by placing food in our mouth. We hardly had a chance to eat our own food before it was scooped up and a large mouthful was shoved in our mouth. There was a lot of laughter, pats and hugs as we ate. We had a band play music as we ate and some youngsters started dancing. Tasneem and I both liked to dance, and we had planned a wedding dance so after we finished our meal, we had to be a little rude and ignore people wanting to come and chat to us. Tasneem's brother announced that we would do the wedding dance and people got off the dance floor and let us have the centre stage. He played the music that we had chosen. Tasneem had made me watch a beautiful Indian Bollywood love story and played the songs from that movie so many times. I liked the song she wanted us to dance to. We had practised and did a fusion dance of Bollywood, a sort of salsa and a waltz, and so we started the dance, people watched until we got into the waltz and then we got everyone to join in. Popa came and took Tasneem from me and they danced, her parents would not dance, but both of her siblings joined in and danced with me and my siblings in a circle.

We went to cut the cake and then left our guests to dance as we made sure we had greeted all our elders. Some of the guests then left early, but our closest friends, some colleagues who had never experienced such a wedding and family stayed and danced. Tasneem and my sons regularly take out our wedding album and make their mum tell them about that day in detail from the start of the Nikaah, the reception and to the photos we had of the honeymoon of us with Umayma. I sit and pretend not to be interested, but I love watching them, correct the odd detail Tasneem was telling them or add details she had missed out; we would pretend to argue and disagree and this made our sons ask more questions, and they begin to correct us as if they had been at our wedding. They had heard the stories so many times, they knew every detail of that weekend as if they were auspicious guests present at every moment!

I heard Tasneem utter a high pitched, howling wolf scream; it suddenly got crazy in my hospital room. Tasneem's parents had arrived with my sons. While they were talking and catching up, my youngest son, Noor, grabbed my hand and pulled it, telling me to wake up. He told me that he was leaving nursery and going to the primary school for big boys and didn't I want to see him dressed in his new school uniform? He was begging me to wake up and his older brother, my darling Ismail, scolded him, but then he also put his mouth close to my ears and quietly begged me to wake up. He ended by saying how much he missed me, but Mum missed me more. My sons broke my heart, but it was exactly the catalyst I needed. I opened my eyes. I saw all the tubes and my throat was so painful; I tried to talk and almost choked or was I drowning? Tasneem saw; she started to scream for help, and my room was flooded with health professionals. Tasneem shouted at her parents, who looked terrified, to take the children and get them some drinks. Her mum held each of my son's hands and pulled them out of my room. I could hear my younger son crying loudly and my older son asked if daddy was dying as they left the room.

Chapter 4
Recovery

I was calmer, but the specialist was explaining what had happened, but he was talking too fast and all he was doing was frightening me. I was so confused. Tasneem told him to stop talking and asked me to look into her eyes filled with tears, oh those huge liquid chocolate-like eyes! She then gently, slowly explained that they were going to take the tube out of my throat and see if I could breathe on my own. I blinked and she told the consultant and nurse to do it, but to be extremely careful and gentle as if I was one of her children receiving the care. I had never been a patient in a hospital; I thought I was a considerate surgeon, but all this was making me rethink how I behaved with my patients. It was more frightening than I had ever imagined, the pain was intense, and when the tube came out, I thought my insides were on fire. I was panicking so much I had held my breath, then I thought I was choking, but these were feelings after months of not using my normal breathing mechanisms. I tried to talk, but no words came out. Tasneem told me to sip some warm water and this was soothing, but I struggled to swallow and the water dribbled out of my mouth. I also kept crying with strange animalistic grunts and pitch and didn't understand why I sounded so bizarre. I was alive and should be happy, but I felt unhappy, had immense and intense fear that I would spend the rest of my life being unable to move or speak. I looked at Tasneem, she had lost weight and looked worried, though she was masking it with her smile, but her eyes gave her away. She also looked scared and fearful.

I couldn't help it, I cried, grunted and there were spasms of terror and joy mixed with fear of being stuck like this. Tears were flowing from Tasneem's eyes now and one of the nurses, who I recognised from her smell, she also smelled of the same perfume she had worn when she tended to me in my coma state. She took over and tried to calm me down. I thought I was calm, but my body could not be controlled, it had shut down for too many months, but I was now aware of what was happening. I had to teach my brain to lead again. I had been in a coma for months and didn't even know why I was crying and making some very odd and strange sounds. I think it was the relief of simply being alive and awake. I was alive! I couldn't remember why I had been in a coma. I remembered memories of a car accident, was this real or had I made it up? No, the police had come and talked about me having been attacked with a knife. Did that happen? Tasneem held my hand. She kept stroking my arm, and I was starting to calm down, but why couldn't I speak? I wondered if I had a stroke and tried to ask Tasneem. Maybe this was why the words didn't come out of my mouth? The lovely nurse with the smell I liked was now talking, very slowly. Explaining that as I had a tube, being intubated to help me breath, my throat would be sore for a few days. She needed me to keep sipping water, to try to not talk and to keep staying calm. I didn't understand why everyone kept telling me to stay calm, I was 'Mr Calm' after all. Mum soon returned and this helped. She wiped my mouth and brow, stroked me and put an arm around Tasneem who could not stop the tears flowing down her face. Popa came next and kissed my forehead, and as his face came close to mine, I saw his eyes brimming with tears. I had not seen him cry since his parent's funerals.

My in-laws returned with my sons, who had been so afraid, they needed to see that their daddy had not died. I even saw relief in Tasneem's father's eyes, which were also filled with tears. I was trying to swim out of the confusion and fog clouding my mind and remembered that the days when my father-in-law did not trust me had happened a long time ago and he no longer felt the same. He now saw me as a good son-in-law; we met at family gatherings and he always put his arm around me like he saw Popa did. I think he even likes me nowadays. I tried to smile, but I had no idea if my body did anything I asked of it. My sons were raised and kissed me; I didn't even have the strength to hug them or raise my hand to pat their heads or touch their face. Tasneem could see they were still frightened of a body in a bed that looked like a very thin version of their daddy, but this person no longer acted like the daddy they loved, so she asked her parents to take my sons home after she had hugged, kissed and reassured them that their daddy was very much alive and he would not die. I did not want them to leave and started to cry again, but this only frightened them as I was making those strange animalistic noises. Mum came and patted my arm and stroked my hair.

My eldest sister Remi and her husband came later bringing Gulshan and her husband. My mum had told me how my two wonderful sisters had lately fallen out, as usual, over nothing important at all. There had been shouting; Remi could be very aggressive and nasty; Gulshan was over-sensitive and always gave in, but reacted by not talking to her older sister. My situation had not only got them talking, but made them closer than ever. Their children were happy because now they could attend family events and socialise with each other again, something they were not allowed to do when the two sisters fell out. A rift would cause the whole family to suffer. They all cried when they saw me awake, hugged, kissed and fussed over me, but I knew I looked dreadful. I kept crying and this strange howling sound kept coming out of my mouth; Mum went to the other side of me from Tasneem and helped her clean me. She had brought Zamzam water, which is blessed and comes from a special religious fountain from Mecca. She used a teaspoon to help me take small sips. Then she rubbed honey on sore lips, also blessed from Mecca. I tried to lick my lips, but this proved impossible. Mum mixed some honey with the Zamzam water and I sipped this. I was now much more relaxed; my eyes had shut and I had fallen asleep.

I woke, and it was dark; Mum was sleeping on a blow-up mattress on the floor, and Tasneem was curled up in her sleeping bag on the chairs. She had gone home to shower and change; normally, she would not have returned until the morning, but she was afraid that I would wake and panic if I was left on my own even though Mum offered to stay. She knew all this had been too much for my mum. She needed a good night's sleep, but she had got more and more stubborn, but she had been proven right that I would recover and the machines should not be turned off. This had made her more determined and assertive. She refused to leave my side. I slept on and off; I felt so exhausted and knew this was ridiculous because from what I understood, I had done nothing but sleep over the last six or more months. As it was the weekend, my sons came to visit again. Tasneem had cleaned me and changed me from the hospital gown to some pyjamas which looked huge on me. I did not cry, and they looked less scared. I still could not talk, could not eat, but managed to sip water, and had some milk with a protein powder that would help to build my strength. I was also drip-fed, which had kept me alive all these months. Tasneem's mum brought a light and thin broth that she said would also help to begin to build my strength. Gulshan was there with her two children and the four children played for a while to the disapproval of the nurses who complained there were too many people in the room. I was so happy to have them all there, still confused, but the noise of the children and the chatter of the adults was comforting. I knew that these were no longer dreams. Remi came next with her family.

I saw Tasneem turn fiery; Remi and her husband quickly got the children ready; she came and kissed me and said Mum and Popa were coming after lunch. No jibe, no sarcastic comment or dig, who was this person? I saw the anxiety in her eyes; I was trying to smile, but a grunt came out instead. I saw her wipe the tears from my eyes; she kissed me again and said she would see me on Sunday and left taking my sons with her. Tasneem's fury was aimed at the two white police officers who came in uninvited, dressed in suits followed by a black policewoman in uniform who even I noticed looked afraid. Tasneem was telling them to go away, but they came up to me. Why were they here? I had heard Tasneem say something about me having almost died; she mentioned a knife. I was confused, I still believed I had been involved in a car accident or would rather believe that then the thought that someone wanted to kill me and had nearly managed it. The man dressed in a suit asked me some questions, but nothing was clear. I closed my eyes; it was too much, what was he saying? Tasneem spoke firmly and loudly and told them it was much too soon; she almost had to physically push them out of the room, and I heard the door slam. They kept coming every few days. My lovely mum, who has never been rude to anyone, actually pushed them out of the room one day during the following week. Mum looked older than I had ever seen her. What was going on?

I was desperate to get out of bed and wanted so badly to have a shower; I wanted to feel hot water run down my body. A lovely male nurse had come in almost every day and helped Tasneem give me a bed bath, but I never felt clean and smelled funny. I asked Tasneem. I was speaking clearly, or so I thought, and she said a few words asking, "Do you want to eat saag, soup?" All that was coming out of my mouth was s.s.se.se.se. The frustration brought tears to my eyes, and she wiped my eyes and gently told me not to worry. I saw her think deeply, and she asked if I was telling her if I could get out of bed? I nodded. "Do you want to start to use the bathroom?" I nodded, and she smiled and asked, "Do you want a shower?" I sort of smiled. The nurse was having none of it, but Tasneem refused to be prevented from helping me do what I wanted. Remi and her husband had come to visit, and they said they would leave when Mum and Popa arrived to stop the nurses from constantly getting annoyed by us. Tasneem asked for their help to get me into a wheelchair. I didn't want my sister's help, but Tasneem said she couldn't do it by herself. The three of them placed me gently in a wheelchair, but I couldn't sit up. My body had lost most of the muscle mass; there was no fat at all, and I seemed to have lost all my strength. My brother-in-law held me upright whilst Tasneem wheeled me to the bathroom. Thank goodness, I had my own room, the perks of being a well-known surgeon! Remi did not enter the bathroom. They moved me to the plastic seat inside the shower; Tasneem took off my pyjamas and used the hand shower whilst Rahim held me upright. The feeling was as if I was on some hot island under a waterfall. I felt the hot water and opened my mouth to let the water run in and out. Tasneem scrubbed and sponged my back, my legs; she cleaned every part of me thoroughly. They raised me, and I tried to stand, but this was impossible. They dried me, and I felt so much better and could smell myself; I smelled lovely!

My nephew came to visit the next day and brought his iPad; he suggested I try to type in order to write on the keyboard what I wanted to 'talk' to us. With Tasneem holding my hand, I could ask and speak better through typed words. I typed and asked, "What happened, what?" She told me that the police wanted me to remember without me being prompted, and both they and the psychotherapist who was monitoring my progress thought it would be better for me to try to think and remember what had happened without being told. I nodded, then typed, "I heard you, knife, murder?" She nodded but would not say anymore. I typed and asked, "Was it Mimi?" Tasneem told me they weren't sure, but the police were interviewing her and her father. I was exhausted and dozed off. The physiotherapist came next; he wanted to assess me and planned some easy exercises to help me start to move better by myself. Everything continued to be so exhausting. A specialist came to talk about my diet. I needed to put on weight and then start to exercise more. Sitting up was a struggle, but I could see improvements and felt stronger day by day. As the weeks passed, I could sit on my own and walk a few steps when I had support and was helped up. We went out with Tasneem pushing me in the wheelchair and my younger son, Noor, loved sitting on my lap when we went out. I was starting to talk; it was odd, broken and disjointed, but now comprehensive especially to Tasneem and even my sons chatted to me, patiently waiting for me to answer using one word and running around the wheelchair in excitement as if all this was normal.

I had never liked dessert and had sweets only occasionally, but now I love ice cream. It was so soothing when my throat was sore and I wanted to eat it at least once a day. I liked the sugar rush and always felt it gave me energy. I was still struggling to gain weight so they were happy to give me any food that I liked. They gave me sleeping tablets to help me sleep as I kept getting up every few hours and in terror but could not remember what made me so afraid. So now I slept over ten hours and insisted Tasneem go home. She and Mum wanted me home, so they were making preparations for this. They converted the second downstairs sitting room into my temporary bedroom and the downstairs bathroom was turned into a wet room for me. I loved our home and was saddened about this, but if it meant I could go home sooner, then it had to be done. The police came again twice. I could say a few words but was now able to write easily. Sadly, I still had no recollection of what had happened.

Visitors kept coming, all my colleagues and specialists had been to visit and look at my notes, making helpful suggestions to help my recovery. I had been lucky, apart from a deep wound into my liver, and two stabs to my back had touched my spinal cord but had done no damage. Tasneem told me I had the best care; a consultant had flown in from Denmark to repair the damage to my liver and associated blood vessels. Most of the deterioration to my health was the result from an infection that ravaged my body as I recovered from the surgery and that had caused the specialist to place me in an induced coma. This affected my heart, and for a while, I was in a vegetative state and brain damage was feared. All the specialists now said I would recover fully, but none had hope before. It was the infection that had damaged me the most, but my body had fought this infection, but it had come back stronger, and the health professionals all had feared the worst. I was determined to get better fully now and prove them all wrong, forget the past and recover quickly and get back to my old healthy self. It was only Tasneem's persistence and resilience that had kept me alive all these months; she refused to let them turn off the machines keeping me alive; they thought I was gone and were asking her about using my organs for donation. She had never let me down, and I was going to do the same and not let her down now. Everyone praised her when they visited, telling me that she had never given up hope and had never left my side. I vaguely remember discussions she had with others about me. I typed and said a few words to thank Tasneem. I told her that I am sure I could hear all the things she was saying when I had been in a coma, all the fights she had to keep me alive and help me get better. She came close to me and kissed me on my lips. Nowadays, she was never shy or coy; she had even kissed me in front of her own father several times, as he had come and kissed my forehead, patted me and sat holding my hand.

I was desperate to go home, but the hospital wanted me to get a little stronger and at least walk with crutches before they would discharge me. All my family would exercise my legs, massage, stretch and bend them when they visited both when I was in a coma and now. Every visitor came with food and Tasneem took her time to feed me; she helped me to the toilet and showered me every day now. I knew I loved her, but what I felt for her now was more profound and overwhelming. She never complained and was gentle but often had to tell me off. She made me push myself, when I cried uncontrollably and made my mum, her mum and even our fathers cry, she refused to cry and refused to give up. She worked so hard. She would leave to check patients in paediatrics, even though she was on compassionate leave, she never came to visit without making sure our sons had their breakfast and their bags ready for school; she never missed any of their events in school and took videos to share with me. She often went home to cook and eat with the boys and then returned in the late evening to sit with me, helped me exercise, to talk and to spend time with me before I drifted off to sleep. I felt she stayed longer watching me sleep, left only when she was certain I was deeply asleep and only then did she go home.

One night, I suddenly woke up at about 3 am in the morning. I had clear visions and my memory of what had happened to me returned. I managed to ring the emergency bell and two nurses came. I was in such a state, they had to calm me and were thinking of sedating me, but I quietened down, was peaceful, nodded and pleaded for them not to do that. I patiently asked for Tasneem. They told me the time. They listened to me say, "Urgent, please, call her, urgent!" They saw that I was relaxed, and it was urgent; they called the doctor who was on call; he came and checked me, listened to me and agreed to let them telephone Tasneem. Of course, she was terrified that something had happened but took no convincing or asked for no explanation when she learned I had woken up agitated and had asked to get her to come in at once. She asked her sister to come to look after her children and she was with me within the hour.

She came and kissed me, which made me feel so much better straight away. She helped me sip some water first and then asked if I was all right. I told her I remembered. I saw a face. I think I knew who had hurt me. She asked if she should call the police and I said yes but in the morning. She said she would send a text and ask them to come as soon as they are able to in the morning. I said I was sorry to wake her, but I needed her, and she smiled. We had been together now through the whole recovery, and she laughed she wasn't going to miss the finale. She got into bed with me; the nurse came to check on us but did not interrupt. This was the first night we had spent next to each other in months since I had woken from my coma. It reminded me of our wedding night.

We were awake at about 6 am. Tasneem went and got us some breakfast and helped me eat; I made her eat, and after she cleared up, she suggested that I type up a statement with her help on the iPad. I agreed. It took much longer than we expected. She helped me get up, washed and I was just returning to the bed and the police arrived. Tasneem did not speak or interrupt but let me tell them. My speech was slow so I told them that I had written a statement, and they were pleased. They read everything, but I was starting to get tired, so they suggested that Tasneem email them my statement, they would print it and I could sign it later. They also wanted me to describe my attacker after I rested and later on in the day they would return with someone who could produce an image of the person I described and would this be alright. I nodded. The recollections were making me feel pain; I wasn't sure if it was physical, emotional or mental, but I dozed off; it was a fitful sleep with dreams and nightmares. I wasn't up to seeing the police again that day and instead met them the next day. I asked Tasneem to please take me home now. We went home two days later.

As we all thought would happen, my recovery was much faster when I went home. I still had to come to the hospital for physiotherapy and check-ups, but I was doing much better than anyone anticipated. My speech improved; I could get in and out of bed alone, could manage to use the bathroom and shower in the wet room. I did not take any risks, and we made sure there was someone, usually Tasneem and my mum or Popa, nearby because if I fell then the consequences were not worth thinking about. Within six months, I managed to walk without crutches but at home. Outside, I was still a little afraid so I used a walking stick for support, but in time, this was not needed. I was able to eat normally and play with my sons. They and Tasneem were my healing medicine and cure; they spurred me to ignore pain, pushed me to the edge of pain in order for the necessary improvements; they gave me the energy and impetus I always needed to succeed fully in my recovery.

Chapter 5
The Knife

Tasneem and I had decided to work four days a week when our first son Ismail was born. We had paid fully for the house, even helped to pay off her parents' home; we had enough money and life was wonderful so we wanted to enjoy being a family. I knew Tasneem also wanted to do more than just work and be a mum, daughter and sister. Our first year of marriage had been heady and manically busy. We liked visiting family and friends, travelled extensively and had a filled social life full of parties and dinners. We walked, swam and she had started me cycling without being afraid. We would put our baby Ismail in his special seat on the back of my bike and cycled miles, picnicked and got to know the UK better. We went to Europe and planned going further when Ismail was older, though we were already planning to take him to Malaysia. Then Tasneem got pregnant again and life continued to improve but was even more hectic, but working four days a week helped us to have quality family time. I thought I would never be able to let go of all my work commitments, but it was very easy. Tasneem felt the same; she took off six months after having each of our sons; she consulted and would take her baby into work but did no more work than that. She loved being a mummy and I loved being a daddy.

We had friends who had near-death experiences either from accidents or horrible illnesses like cancer. We remembered conversations of 'I wish I had time to do XYZ', but when they recovered, the same people who wished for better lives, often reverted to their extremely busy lives, never really having time to enjoy the fruits of their labour, their family or friends. We had male friends who were angry at fighting for custody battles, yet I remember having spoken to the same men telling them to be better husbands and fathers when they were still married, spend more time with family, but they ignored this. Then thousands were spent fighting the very person they had said they loved, winning some contact with the children but then leaving the very children they had fought to have quality time with nannies or their own elderly parents as they were too busy at work to spend time with the children. Tasneem and I had moments of disagreement, but we made a huge effort to talk, share, communicate and work our way through difficult issues. It was too easy to argue, feel always in the right, to throw tantrums and anger towards those closest to us. Tasneem would always get on her bike and 'run away' during heated conversations, then she would return calmer and want to talk, and apologise far too quickly, Instead she would bring up the issues during quieter times, so we could talk through the issues. She called cycling her therapy, but I worried as she did crazy things when she was annoyed or angry and this made me feel more remorseful, as if anything were ever to happen to her, I knew my world would be shattered.

My one hatred of a word is for the word 'busy'. Too busy on the mobile phone, watching television, sitting in a pub whilst the family struggled, spouses felt lonely, unappreciated and angry. My family argued and disagreed, but we put in effort never to put each other down and hold grudges, and my sisters, in particular, often failed at this. I remembered how patient my parents had been with Tasneem's father and had done their utmost best to get him on side when I wanted to marry her. It had not been easy, even today there were times that he disapproved, and we let him. He had a right to his views, but we also patiently tried to explain our point of view, often agreeing to disagree and not get angry. I could easily have avoided Tasneem's father, but what would this have achieved? He had raised Tasneem; he was her father no matter what and deserved respect for this alone. It was clear he loved my sons, and had I avoided him, they and he would have missed out. Both Tasneem and I read every book on various therapies, Psychology and communication. We learned to give in when issues did not matter and allow different views when it did. We listened to everyone and respected all views, though we did not often agree, everyone had a right to comment. We believed that often it was best to simply let go, unless it really mattered, only then was it worth fighting and proving you were in the right.

Any time Tasneem came into work, she would bring me lunch if I was at the hospital on those same days, and of course, she planned it so that it was exactly so and she made sure we saw each other at least once at work on those days. She would come laden with lunch, often not just for me but for my PA or one of the colleagues who was close friends with us. Once, I was standing outside my office talking to a new staff member and Tasneem came carrying Ismail in a sling and I could already smell the food. Before I spoke, my colleague piped up and said that my nanny was here. I looked at him and then at Tasneem. We had had this happen a few times. I hadn't really thought much about our colour difference; Tasneem was to me only slightly darker than me and she looked like the classic, beautiful women found in India and East Africa. In the summer, she loved being out in the garden or the park with the baby on the bike and she tanned easily. I thought I did too, but I was much paler than her and so people thought, at times, that she was the nanny. It made me annoyed, but usually Tasneem found it amusing. She shared stories of how often patients went to consult with white nurses and ignored her, the one in charge, or other doctors and consultants just because they were people of colour. Tasneem hated that every staff member now went around in scrubs; she found it lazy and unprofessional as it made everyone appear to be the same status. Some of the details on the nurses' old uniforms were fussy, frilly or pointless, but modern uniforms were functional and comfortable. Nowadays, there was an expectation that a hospital had to provide scrubs for all. Tasneem was always getting vomited on by children or covered in something unpleasant hence scrubs were often essential to her work, but it made other people always class her as inferior when she was dressed in her scrubs. She had never found a colleague of hers to do this to her, make an assumption, but some patients did. She had clearly heard my colleague refer to her as my nanny but she ignored him, did not show her upset and instead, rather loudly called me darling and kissed me on the lips which she rarely did in public. I could tell and knew she was very annoyed. Normally, she would have invited any of my colleagues talking to me to come eat with us, but she just passed us and marched into my office. I didn't bother saying goodbye and left my dumbfounded colleague standing alone, looking at us and feeling foolish. It was only during my long time in a coma in hospital did Tasneem finally forgive him. He visited often, always bringing Tasneem the chai she liked; he would make it himself and bring it piping hot, saying little to her, but he would sit next to me talking of the cases he was dealing with and gave Tasneem a chance to have a break.

We, now, never worked on Fridays and would go away as soon as we could leave London Thursday night or as early as possible on the Friday. Our favourite journey was to visit my parents and there would always be someone else visiting at the same time. They loved to babysit, so we went for long walks, or the four or more of us took Ismail to visit a National Trust property, or when the weather was fine, we drove to the nearest seaside and met even more families and friends there. We had been thinking about buying a home for all the family near the sea and Popa was doing research and looking for the right property. However, one week as I had needed to complete some reports before leaving for the weekend to see my parents, I had cycled early to the NHS hospital. I thought I would be done by lunchtime so we could leave London and miss the Friday traffic. Our youngest son, Noor, was turning five at the weekend and my parents wanted to host his birthday party. They had invited all of Tasneem's family, my family and a few close friends who had children. We would collect the boys from school and nursery, then drive down to them. Once there, we would start cooking the food and decorate the house and garden. Popa told me he had bought a large trampoline, had it all set up, so we were all excited about seeing it and were looking forward to meeting everyone.

I was engrossed in my work and deep in thought. There was a knock at the door to my office at the NHS hospital and I was still thinking about the weekend. I asked the person to come in, but no one entered. They knocked again, and I got up to open the door. I recognised the man, but wasn't sure from where. I smiled and was about to ask him to come in and what he wanted, but he lunged at me. He had a knife, and I felt it enter my chest or the side of my body. He was fast, and I used my hands to defend myself as he repeated his attack and cut my hand and arm. I felt something warm, a liquid coming out of my shirt and spreading like an ink stain on blotting paper. He said I had killed his mother, but I had no idea what he was talking about. He told me how I had destroyed all their lives; his dad was depressed; he had ended up breaking up with his girlfriend as his father had become so needy. I collapsed to the floor. The man kicked me, and I tried to roll over into a ball in the foetal position to instinctively protect myself. I felt the warm blood pouring out of me; I was covered in blood and realised it was all my own blood. He bent down and stabbed me again in my back, and I lost consciousness.

He hadn't been able to shut the door properly when he left and one of my colleagues knocked when she saw my door open and then tried to enter my room when no one answered and saw me immediately in a pool of blood. I had tried to call out but couldn't move. She shouted, then screamed and called for help. She didn't move me but felt a pulse and screamed out orders, saying I was alive; she got help, found a scarf and pressed it on the wound to my side that was oozing blood too fast, this was the cut to my liver. I felt arms lift me onto a trolley and could only see corridor after corridor as I was rushed to the emergency ward.

Tasneem told me my colleague had saved my life; she was covered in my blood from helping me, but if she had walked on, I would have bled to death, so I was lucky she found me minutes after the stabbing and these crucial minutes saved me. They had seen the man on CCTV from the hospital cameras but not clearly enough and no one had been able to identify him. They had operated on me for eight hours to stop the blood loss and fix my liver. I was operated again the next day; this time a specialist who was in London from Denmark was called to help mend the main vessel that had ruptured in my liver. He had managed to sew it and repair the extensive damage. I needed several pints of blood transfusion, and they were still not sure if I would survive.

I caught an infection two days later and the best cause of action was to put me in an induced coma that would help my body heal and recover with antibiotics being pumped into me intravenously and stop the infection spreading to all my internal organs. Tasneem and my family were told to expect the worst, and this happened two weeks later. The specialist said he thought I was brain dead when he came to check up on me whilst I was in the coma and thought the best cause of action was to turn off the machines which undoubtedly kept my brain alive and my heart pumping. Tasneem did not agree. She told me that my parents and her parents told her to listen to the experts, but she knew that we, the medical professionals, occasionally made mistakes and she wanted to wait. She knew me and knew I would fight to stay alive. She had persisted and was correct, I hadn't left her yet. I asked how she knew that I would live and she said she just knew.

She knew my strength, resilience and my love for her and the family. She knew I was not ready to leave her just yet and that I would fight if I was given a chance.

The police came after I had eaten a tiny bit of breakfast. I was still struggling to eat. They wanted me to think about the man, so I told them I recognised him. After I told them what he said, they got the record of all the females who had passed away and in my fifteen years, they were surprised that there were not that many female patients who had died after I did surgery on them and were in my care. I generally did standard types of surgery, but they all carry risks. I had a vague recollection of a woman who was an alcoholic, obese and we had told her she needed to lose weight before we could operate on her, otherwise we would have lost her during the surgery or not been able to even do the surgery on her. I told the police to check this particular case.

They had already asked me about Mimi; Tasneem and my family had shared with the police all the awful things she had done; they had some of it on record and Tasneem had given consent to them accessing the files held by my solicitor. They had been focused on her and having interviewed my colleagues no one remembered the case of this particular woman and thus had made no links to her son who stabbed me. I remembered how he hadn't wanted me to operate on his mother and heard him say that he didn't want a 'foreigner' operating on his mother. My colleague who was white had said that his parents came from Poland and Sweden, whereas I was born in England, educated and studied at the best universities, so it was either me who operated or he could take his mother elsewhere as we did not tolerate racist behaviour. The son had gotten very angry and punched the wall, but he knew it was not safe to move his mother, so he had relented. I had operated on her, and it had gone very well. The police went to my colleagues to ask more about the case, and when they asked about that particular case, one colleague said he did remember it clearly and managed to find the notes, and of course, they had the son's address as the next of kin.

After the operation had gone to plan on the woman, she was discharged, but the woman had not taken care of herself as she had been instructed and died a month later. Her son came and yelled at me, blaming me for her death, and security guards came and escorted him out. He put in several complaints about me and accused me of killing his mother because she was fat and white. He wrote more complaints to the Board of Directors, the General Medical Council, to his MP and to the Ombudsman, but there was no case for me to answer. I had done nothing wrong; her death was attributed to a heart attack by a white forensic pathologist. She had started to smoke and drink alcohol after giving them up to have the operation and did not stick to the diet prescribed to maintain her health. Her body simply could not cope. I found my car scratched, and I kept seeing him. I should have complained and reported him to the police then, but he suddenly stopped stalking me. I thought about reporting him and was advised by the hospital to do so, but fearing this might start his harassment of me all over again, I didn't make a counter complaint. Tasneem said that if he came anywhere near the family, she would complain, but nothing happened, and we forgot about him. He waited and attacked me a year later. We do not know why he waited so long, maybe he had spent the time complaining or planning it, and when nothing worked, he took it upon himself to punish me then?

The police identified him and got a warrant for his arrest. They went to the flat he lived in with his father. He was nowhere to be found. They discovered that his father had passed away from natural causes, but when they questioned the neighbours, they shared that this had really accelerated his anger. He always told everyone about the Paki foreigner who had killed his mother and now his father. The police couldn't find my attacker. They investigated my attacker and found that this man had been angry most of his life; he was always skipping school, moved from job to job and had periods of unemployment. He was openly a member of the National Front and moved from various political and right-wing movements that shared his values. Further investigations showed that he might have travelled abroad.

Being told this, none of it helped and made me feel depressed. I had never turned down helping anyone, yes, we needed many of our patients to change their lifestyle; obesity, alcohol and smoking were serious issues that made it impossible to help patients improve the chance of longevity. My patient and her husband seemed to understand, and she already looked much better when she came for her operation just by losing several stones in weight. Her husband told me he was proud of his wife; they were now walking every evening and my recommendations had helped them both already improve the quality of their lives. Her death was just bad luck, or the way she has lived most of her life was just too strong a pull and she had reverted back to her bad habits. The son should have asked his family doctor for support, to explain, and I am sure the hospital would have given him information about support groups and how to maintain good health for his parents when he saw that they were struggling.

I suppose it was easier for him to blame me and to lash out. His hatred did not need much fuel to push him to the edge.

The police had found the knife he used in the attack in the bread bin in the kitchen of the flat; it had taken them a thorough search to find it because the flat had been in an awful state. I wonder why he hadn't thrown it away. They had had a puppy; nothing had been cleaned, not even the puppy's mess, and letters showed that the council were trying to evict the man. He had many months head start, and they had found that he had bought a train ticket on the Eurostar train to France about two months ago. I think this was about the time I came out of a coma; he probably thought I had died, and the BBC had done a Crimewatch program about my attack and then the news had covered that I was alive and recovering. The man must have seen this and gone on the run. CCTV identified him in hospital the day of my attack, the Police had now been able to make a definitive match. Although the knife had been cleaned, they found my DNA on the grooved and serrated edges of the knife as evidence that that was the weapon used on me, and his fingerprints proved that he was the perpetrator of the attack on me.

He was eventually found in Slovenia. He had joined the Far Right there and been arrested for attacking some immigrants during a fascist demonstration. When the police there checked his records, they found the warrant for his arrest from the UK, and he was brought to England within a week of being arrested in Slovenia, which was part of the EU and so complex extradition was not required. We did not go to his sentencing hearing, thank goodness, he had pleaded guilty so taxpayers' money was not wasted on a trial to prove his crime. He boasted and was proud to say he had almost killed a Paki.

The police had also charged Mimi and her father for their crimes against me, but now, all they were charged with were theft and malicious damage. The police wanted me to make a statement, but one attack was hard enough, and I no longer wanted to think about Mimi and the awfulness I had experienced with her all those years ago. Also she had admitted what she had done when she heard of my impending death and swore neither she nor her family were the one who attacked me. It had scared her. The police kept insisting that I press charges against Mimi, but I would not oblige. I was exhausted and recovering; I would rather invest my energy in getting better as quickly as possible rather than be vindictive and full of hate over something that was part of my forgotten past.

When I finally returned to my office, one of the administrative staff came to greet me. I had seen them all either whilst I recovered in hospital or when they visited us in our home. I wondered what she wanted. She said that about a month ago, a man and a woman had left some parcels and a letter for me. She hadn't wanted to take them, but they said it was urgent, had asked if they ought to take it to my home and had my previous address, but she did not want to tell them where I now lived. I was glad she heeded data protection as I did not want strangers knowing where I lived with my family. Anyway, she said they had insisted and insisted, swore they were things I would want and there was nothing dangerous or harmful so she had taken the things they wanted to leave for me. I said it was fine and she could bring the parcels to me.

I thought I would be afraid to go back into my office, but I felt nothing. Of course, it had been cleaned and there were no signs of the attack. I had told the hospital to give my office to another colleague, but out of respect, they had not done this. As they knew I was coming in that day, my office had been cleaned and I noticed that it had been newly painted. There was new furniture and someone had bought me teabags, milk, some biscuits; there was a vase on my desk full of fresh flowers and a basket of fruit. I was lost in my thoughts, and there was a knock at my door and my secretary came with the administrative staff carrying some parcels. I recognised Mimi's handwriting, and I was wondering if I ought to open them or call the police, but one of the parcels was clearly that of a wrapped painting, had she returned what she had stolen from me? I called Tasneem on video call and together we would open everything. After opening the painting, I realised that I had been correct. I then opened a small parcel with a letter attached. There was a small box inside, and I gasped in surprise to find that these were my grandfather's cufflinks. I felt a mixture of sorrow and joy as I had not seen them in years. The letter contained a cheque for twenty thousand pounds and a note that simply said, "Sorry and thank you for not pressing charges." Well, my name meant 'compassionate and merciful' after all. I learned never to hold grudges and revenge led to nothing good. I did not bother to open the other parcels and chatted to Tasneem instead. She said she believed that Mimi had finally done the correct thing. I was about to tear up the cheque, but Tasneem said she thought it would be better to invest it in our Malaysian projects and what did I think of that? She told me to not worry, not to make any rash decisions and she would meet me for lunch later on to discuss this further. I held the cufflinks in my hand and slipped them into my pocket next to my heart. I put away the cheque and decided to forget Mimi for now.

Tasneem and I always talked about how lucky we were to have close family and friends, but none of them were white and English; we had Tim, who was Scottish, and his family, lots of acquaintances from work, school, but none, for example, ever popped in or were so close to us that we did the same. When we both lost our grandparents, we found that the people we considered to be close friends to us, stayed away, did not talk about our loss, some even said they did not know what to say or do so did nothing! Our community, friends from abroad and other parts of the UK sent flowers, cards, telephoned, asked if we needed anything and inundated us with support, food, chat and kindness. Tim and Fiona came with the children, specially, to offer condolences all the way from Scotland. I remembered one of my senior bosses got embarrassed when he asked how I was, and I actually started to tell him how my grandma, my daddima had died. I saw and felt a nervousness; he looked at his watch and fidgeted like a child needing the toilet. I stopped talking, ended the conversation and we each went off on our way. This was not the only occasion this happened. Tasneem and I found similar experiences throughout our life. Conversations happened, but they were superficial. There were definitely cultural variations, distance and behaviours depending on who we talked to, if it was about sad or difficult experiences, and those we thought of as our dear friends, we discovered, were not the people we imagined them to be at a time of need.

Chapter 6
School

My colleagues and Tasneem never understood why I refused to see a patient in my room alone. I didn't understand why anyone would risk doing this. I called a nurse if there was no family member or friend to accompany patients or if they didn't want their family with them during consultations. If possible, I also left the door ajar. I could and would never be over-cautious or take the slightest risks about such things.

My grandfather wanted every grandchild educated privately from primary school onwards, but when it was suggested to me at age eight years, I kicked off, was angry and difficult. My parents could not believe it as I had always been mild mannered, impeccably behaved and hardly had a tantrum as a baby. I was a bit quiet as a child, considered too well-behaved and Popa thought that a private school might toughen me up, but thank goodness, my mum was afraid of my reaction and instead agreed with me. She sympathised with me and wanted to wait until secondary school before I was sent away to private school. I loved being at home with my family. I had listened to Popa and would try to be more of what he wanted, as long as he did not send me away. My sisters always had friends visiting; they were sporty and sociable. I would copy; I started to become more active in primary school, joined a few clubs, even though all I wanted was to go home as soon as school ended. I even auditioned for a part in the school play in my last two years at primary school, got fairly big parts and despite feeling sick with nerves, I participated and loved seeing the pride in my parents and sisters' faces when they came to watch the plays. They talked about the play, my part and my acting for months before, during and after the play finished. My parents bought tickets for as many of the family who wanted to come and see me act. They cheered and people stared at our family, but they did not care as they beamed with pride. I now started to understand. If I did this, perhaps I could stay at home, get into a good school locally and live at home. I worked hard and made sure I continued to be at the top of my class.

I was not just at the top of my class at primary school, I won many of the awards at the school prize giving day for writing the best story in English, getting a hundred per cent in the maths test, writing the best poem and I even won a medal for swimming. The headmaster mentioned that I had obtained a scholarship to the most exclusive school in England and as a result I was awarded the final prize of best pupil of the year award. My parents were immensely proud and I saw, I thought, tears shining in Mum's eyes and Popa had stood up so all could see that he was the father of that child who had done extremely well. I used this to reason with my parents that I no longer get sent away as I had changed, matured and was no longer that shy and reserved child, but there was no discussion. My father had selected a school; we went to look around, I was made to sit the entrance exam and was interviewed for the school, both of which I sailed through. Uniforms were bought and my mum tearfully packed my belongings over the summer.

The long summer holidays were usually joyful; we always rented several homes near the sea that all of the extended family visited; we went to different parts of the UK, France, Spain, Portugal, Slovenia, Italy and once even to the Caribbean. We played, ate together, visited local sites, and it was the happiest time of my life. I tanned and had endless adventures with my cousins. I never wanted the summer holidays to end. However, the summer before I was sent away to boarding school was the worst. I experienced feelings of periodic sadness which I had to hide, and it was one of the most distressing times in my life. I could not relax; the adventures were not as much fun and I had no idea why. I had two older cousins who liked their boarding schools, but I loved my family more. As long as I was home at night, I liked school and worked hard. The thought of being sent away, seeing my family a few times a year over school holidays made me feel ill. I always did what I was asked and instructed, but how I wished I could change my parents' mind. I think my mum felt my concerns, but she always thought Popa knew best and agreed with him on this one decision.

It took almost two hours to drop me to my new school from London. I could have come to the school for a week of summer school, but I begged and begged that I did not need to go. In reality, I did not want to go and had done so well in my primary school, my parents actually agreed that I did not need any more extra learning or tuition. I always read, even on holiday; I was curious and researched the area we visited on vacation, so they knew that I was fine in that respect and did not need to attend a summer school to keep up with my learning. I had not seen the school since I had come for a tour and my interview. I had thought of doing badly in the entrance exam, messing up my interview, but I was never that devious or cruel. I got almost a hundred percent on the entrance exam, answered politely, jovially and intelligently in my interview and even won a scholarship so my parents only had to pay a fraction of the school fees. They were so happy with everything and failed to notice my sadness, fear and distress. They took me to the bedroom; met the other boys and their parents I was to share with. There were four older boys introduced who would be our mentors and support us younger boys on a pastoral level. My mum unpacked some things, reminded me of the treats she had packed and told me there was enough for me to share.

I walked with them to their car after tea and Mum hugged, then kissed me, telling me they would see me in five weeks for a week of half-term holidays. We were allowed to call twice weekly and Mum made me promise not to forget to do that. I nodded, afraid that I would burst into tears if I tried to speak, so I smiled and waved as they drove off. Today was Saturday and we had the rest of the day and Sunday to settle in, sign for extracurricular activities and investigate the school and its grounds. I was relieved that we were allowed to go for walks and decided to do that as I did not want anyone to see how upset I was. The school grounds were huge and beautiful; there were play areas, a heated swimming pool, pitches and courts for every sport imaginable. I later discovered that some boys even took horse riding lessons in nearby stables, but I was just happy to walk and swim. I played hockey in winter and was so happy to be picked for the cricket team in the summer.

On Sunday, the four boys who were meant to look after us, came and made each of us give them a lot of the treats that our mothers had packed for us. I tried to resist and got slapped hard on my head, and without waiting for me, one of the older boys ransacked my chest and took all my chocolate, my mum's wonderful cake that I was going to cut that day and share and threw my Indian snacks into my case out of their containers. When they left, I picked every bit of food and put it back in the container. They did the same to all the five boys I shared with, and we learned they did the same to the boys in the next two rooms. I was seething and wanted to report them, but we were warned not to do this as they left our room. If we did, there would be repercussions and consequences, such that our young minds could not imagine. I still thought about reporting them, I was fearless, but then I thought against doing it. There was no point in rocking the boat this early with bullies as I had seven years to spend in this school. From then on, I ignored them, never greeted them and made sure I was never alone near them. I already disliked them.

Nothing more happened the first week at school. My biggest problem was food. I never thought I was a fussy eater, I love food, but I just could not enjoy the food at the boarding school. It was so bland, and I found everything slightly over cooked. I loved my mum's Lasagne, but when we were served it for dinner one evening, it tasted so dull and the actual pasta was slimy. I thought there was only one way to cook and make food, why did everything taste so bad in the school? My favourite meals of the day were breakfast and high tea. I filled up on a large bowl of cereal, two eggs and toast, then had one slice of toast smothered in strawberry jam, and we had tea in the afternoon with cookies or cake, and I loved this mid-afternoon treat, but we were only given one piece, and it was always delicious but never enough for me. I hardly ate lunch or dinner; I tried really hard to eat as much as I could, but I just did not like what was served. I took the smallest portions and every time thought it would taste better than it did, so I would ask for more, but this never happened. I basically shoved the small amount into my mouth and used milk to help me swallow the food. There were no enticing smells like at home, even Mum's pasta or homemade pizza was delectable and the house would smell of herbs and garlic. In school, all the food had this one smell, and it wasn't the nicest of smells.

On the fifth night of the following week, I could not sleep so I got up to see if I could find some bread. I could never sleep if I was hungry and I was going through my treats Mum had given me far too quickly, especially after the older boys had stolen so much of it. I had resisted eating too much of the remaining treats that night. I always filled up on bread or fruit if there was nothing else to eat. I got out of bed, left my shared bedroom and walked towards the kitchen to get a glass of milk and some bread. As I left my room, I heard some strange noise. One of the doors of the study room was open and I quietly walked towards it. Instead of rushing in, I peeked carefully inside and saw two older boys with a younger boy. I could not clearly see what was happening, but I saw the two older boys close to the young lad, and one of the older boys was holding the young lad tightly. I heard him whimpering and begging them to stop. He sounded terrified and pathetic. I am sure the other larger boy had his trousers around his ankles. I wanted to do something; I wondered where the teachers were and should I go to find the housemaster? I just could not move, the sounds and the crying boy petrified me, and I knew it was important that I not be discovered. I stayed where I was and remained hidden under the table next to the door from which I peeked into the study door periodically. I was angry at my weakness but was terrified of what they might do to me if I were discovered.

I thought I was there for hours, but in actual fact, it was about fifteen minutes. The two older boys laughed, smothered the boy's face and mouth and eventually there was quiet. I checked and quietly but quickly rushed back to my room, careful not to make any sounds. I got into my bed, but I could not stop the shaking. What had they done to the young boy? I had heard that one boy had had his face pushed into the water inside of a toilet the day before because he had stood up to one of the older boys. I thought such stories were myths used to scare younger boys by the older boys, but the headmaster had gathered all the boys in the assembly hall. We had been scolded and told if anything like that ever happened then every boy in the school would be punished. This did not sound fair to me, why were teachers not doing their jobs and making sure all the boys were protected, looked after and safe? Even in my lovely primary school, I had heard of bullying. As it never happened to me, I had never been overly concerned, but now I was thinking about all the stories I had tried to ignore. Should I have talked about our treats being stolen and what I had seen in the study? These were boys who we were told were our mentors; they had been chosen because they were the best, so what would happen if I complained? I decided to say nothing, but I struggled to fall asleep; my hunger was forgotten, but I could not stop remembering the horrible sounds the little boy had been making. I could not and would not forget his weak screams and whimpers.

I struggled to get up the next day. I hardly spoke; I knew a few of the teacher's lost patience with me as I rarely spoke, never answered questions unless I was asked directly, I never volunteered answers and was a solitary soul. I avoided using any of the shared bathrooms; I had found a disabled bathroom that no one used and would sneak into it and lock it. During the day, I avoided any of the quiet areas where the older boys hung around. I spent a lot of time outside but stayed where I knew teachers watched over us. I did the same in the library. In the house meetings, I heard a group of older boys talking about me. They mentioned my looks, I was considered a handsome chap, that I was quiet and never complained so I should be invited into the inner sanctums, but I showed no interest, never attended any exclusive meetings and kept myself to myself. The younger boys stopped trying to be my friends; I was always polite, always answered if asked a direct question but using one-word answers and they thought me aloof or arrogant. I shared none of the chatter about home and families. I was not going to give any of them any information to use against me or to get close to me. I trusted no one. I worked hard, did my homework to a high standard, always researching more than was asked, and I spent all my free time working or walking outside, always with a book. A few of the teachers had tried to talk to me, asked how I was, was I experiencing problems, bullying, but I shook my head and said little. I always got the top marks in tests so there was little they could say to me as I never failed to deliver good work, was never rude and never got into any trouble.

During week three, I was asked to leave my class by a note being delivered to my form tutor and was called to see the deputy headmaster and a nurse. I had been losing a lot of weight, and as I was growing taller, it looked really bad as I had started to look skeletal in the few weeks I had been at school. I had noticed that I was having to tighten my belt on my trousers more but had not been too worried as I always had energy to do what I needed to do. The nurse said that she noticed my weight loss and the eye bags, and they asked if everything was all right. They didn't actually let me answer but talked and talked. They said they understood that I was probably missing home, that this would get better with time, I should join more clubs and not spend so much time reading and being on my own, but do more sports, make friends and build up an appetite. I was thinking about telling them about my treats being stolen, about the abuse of younger children by the older boys, but I wasn't given any opportunity. I hadn't spoken at all! I was sent back to my class.

Later that evening, as I was doing my homework, two of the mentors came and dragged me aside into a room I had never been in. One punched me in the stomach and asked what I had said. I told them I had said nothing, but they did not believe me. One held me and the other started to undo his trousers. I don't know how I managed it, but I pinched and punched the one who was holding me in his private parts, he let go and screamed; the other boy could do nothing as he had his trousers down his knees, and I managed to run out of the room. I left the school building, ran and ran, then hid in the school grounds. I was so cold and shaking with fear. As it started to get dark, I got the courage to go back to the school. I met a teacher outside the main door, and I was such a mess. I was dirty; and he could see I had been crying. I was shaking uncontrollably, and he placed his arm around my shoulders and took me to the nurse. I was too afraid to say anything and just kept asking for my mum. The nurse cleaned me up, wrapped me up warm and fed me some soup, then made me drink tea and gave me a fat slice of cake and a couple of biscuits, which I devoured. My parents arrived soon after. They were shocked to see the state I was in. In three weeks, I was skinny, thin, gaunt and my face had aged.

I knew my parents would believe me if I told them what had happened, but I still could not speak. I was too distressed by potentially being raped to tell my parents this. Popa had shared wonderful stories about his days in his private school, even Mum had liked her time at school though she had been a day-boarder, she went home every night after school. I just asked if they would take me home. Mum stayed and hugged me whilst Popa went to talk to the teachers. Mum spoke gently and told me I could tell her anything; she asked if I was being bullied or if anything terrible had happened to me. I looked into her eyes, a few tears escaped mine and I did not need to say anything. Popa came back and said that they had decided that we all go home tonight and would return to the school on Sunday. I felt huge relief. The housemaster had brought some clean clothes from my room; I changed out of my school uniform and got dressed. I was so happy to go home but sad that I would have to return. Maybe I could convince my parents to let me stay home permanently over the next few days.

Mum sat in the back seat with me, and I fell fast asleep. I do not remember when I had slept so soundly. I awoke the next morning in my own bed; my father and mother had been unable to wake me in the car when we arrived home and together they had carried me to my bed. The next morning, I did not immediately get up but absorbed all the familiar sights and felt so happy. Mum heard me go to the bathroom and came with a tray loaded with food and fruit. There was her homemade muesli and some steaming chai. She sat and watched me eat. I ate and smiled; we kept looking at each other but said nothing and just smiled. She said she would make me toast and eggs when I came downstairs, but I told her I was full. She kept gently touching me; she patted my head lovingly, touched my cheek and my face, and I was reassured. She took my tray and asked me to dress and come downstairs as Popa and she wanted to chat to me.

When I got downstairs, I found them dressed and with their coats on. Mum gave me my jacket, and I put on my shoes as they suggested we go for a walk. I felt happy and safe but did not say anything. Mum held my hand and Popa made small talk and chit chat. It was getting cooler, but I did not care; I was so happy to be home. My mind was racing; I was trying to plan what to say, but I felt stupid as nothing came to my mind. I knew that they knew something was terribly wrong at my school, but my default position was to protect my parents. I did not understand why this was; I knew my parents had seen terrible things in their life, and I knew they wanted to protect me, that I could always trust them, but I just could not tell them everything I saw and heard happen in my few weeks in boarding school. I felt ashamed and cowardly.

Eventually, I asked after my sisters. Mum told me a few of the things I had missed, most of which she and my sisters had already told me when I telephoned home, and then we sat at a table in the park. Mum produced a chocolate bar from her pocket, and I managed to gulp it down. There was hardly anyone around as it was a school day; a few women walked with prams or chatted to other women. I saw that the leaves had fallen off the trees and there was a man sweeping up the leaves from the paths. Popa then asked me to tell them what had happened at school. I just told them that I hated it, I missed them, hated the food and missed my sisters. Popa said this was normal and asked, "Didn't I want to give it a little bit more time?" I shook my head furiously to indicate 'NO!' Mum asked if anything bad had happened and my refusal to talk, told them something unpleasant had happened. I said that I just did not like it there and why couldn't I live at home and go to a grammar school here. Popa said that it was too late to start in another school; they could not find me another school just like that. Did I not appreciate how lucky I was to go to the best school in England? I could see Popa trying hard not to get angry, but he insisted that I had to return to my private school on Sunday, and I begged them again to let me stay home. They asked again to tell them why, what had happened and I said nothing. Mum asked if I would be happier to return as a day boarder. I couldn't see how this would work, we lived too far for me to go back and forth each day. Mum explained that we could rent a house; first, we would stay in a local lodge belonging to the school as they had offered us that. Was that alright with me? My head was buzzing with too many thoughts; my sisters had school walking distance from our home in London, what would happen to them, all our extended family were near, and I wondered if it would be better for me to stay with them instead. How could I be responsible for disrupting my whole family's life. I shared all my concerns. Popa and Mum told me not to worry and they would work everything out. I did worry, and that night, I could not sleep again; I had not managed to eat much for lunch or dinner either.

My sisters jumped on me as soon as I saw them at the school gate when I went with Mum to collect them. I really liked these two naughty kids. They could talk and bicker over the most pointless of disagreements, both usually talking at the same time and listening to no one, but I was glad that they did not interrogate me or expect me to say anything. They told me every detail of everything they had done since I had left for school. Remi told me how she had wanted my bedroom but was told by a stern Mum that I would be back soon and I was not to touch anything in my room. Then they jumped to a story about a child that had wet her pants in sports and pestered Mum about what we were having for dinner. Mum and I smiled at each other; gosh, it was wonderful to be at home. Why could we not just stay like this forever?

After my parents went to bed, I got up and sat outside their room listening to their private conversation. I heard them talking about what was to happen. Popa had decided that my sisters would stay in London with him initially and Mum would return to the lodge with me. He would start looking for a home for the family to rent and then look for new schools for the girls. I was stunned, why would my parents do all this, we were happy in London and why would they change everything? My sisters would get upset; we would move so far from the wider family. Everyone would blame me and hate me. I was shocked and confused.

The next day, we were having lunch at my uncle's home. After everyone had eaten, Popa stood up and told everyone he had news. There was silence as he shared his plans. Like me, everyone was confused, saying that why didn't they just find a school for me in London, why move the whole family away? I was embarrassed as I felt I had created all these problems. I had hoped that like me my parents would have seen the solution was for me to come back home, but Popa explained how the school I had got into was the best school in England and he could not deny me this opportunity. This would open up the world to me; we had all worked so hard to get where we were, we shouldn't give up this easily and at the first hurdle. Everyone talked at once; I hung my head. I should have stood up and told everyone what happened in this prestigious school, but I couldn't say a word. Instead, I looked at my plate trying not to show my anger and my pain; I wanted to cry, but I couldn't even do that. They talked and talked, and I left the table and went into the garden. My cousin came to collect me for dessert and all was calm when I returned, now they were talking about other things, tables were being cleared and tea and dessert were served. My aunt came and put her arm around me, told me not to worry and that everything would be fine. I was given the largest piece of dessert and told to eat up.

When we returned home, Mum started to organise, pack and cook. Popa told her the lodge was fully furnished, but this is what Mum did; she got the three children to help and ordered us to do various things. She also wanted to cook for Popa and my sisters, but he put a stop to that. He reminded her that he could cook, the girls would love to help and he had all the family nearby who, he had no doubt, would send them food as well. He made Mum stop and said we would all watch a movie. We were still full from lunch, and Mum just made a few snacks for us to eat whilst we watched the movie. These were the days I loved; I wish that I hadn't ruined the lunch, but we were back on track; we laughed and oooohed aaaahed at the movie; it was a lovely and easy watch. I often watched my sisters having their eyes glued to the screen, and all felt well and happy. After the movie, Mum helped my sisters get ready for bed. I read whilst Popa watched the news and sports. He talked to me, but mainly, he watched and listened to the television. I was happy in my own world.

Sunday, I was woken to sounds, my aunt and cousins had come to help. Discussions were being had about what to pack and take with us, even though we would be back in two weeks for half-term holidays. They prepared as if we were immigrating, and I wasn't happy to find this on a Sunday morning; normally, we had a huge brunch, went for a walk or to visit family. I was greeted with smiles and pats when I came into the kitchen; there was lots of food ready for me; it seemed I was the last to get up. I ate cereal followed by freshly made paratha and eggs. Mum made me have a bowl of fruit, and I was so full. I am sure my stomach had shrunk at school as I really struggled to eat. I cradled the chai and sat watching everyone being busy, packing and cooking. By midday, everything was ready; we would leave about four in the afternoon, so we even managed a quick walk and then the family came throughout the afternoon to wish us well, bringing snacks, food for us and for Popa. The car was packed, and Mum and I sadly left. I was in a terrible mood; I did not say goodbye; I had been fairly quiet as now all I could think of was going back to school and worried about what the older boys would do to me when they saw me return.

Mum was surprised that I dozed off; when I awoke, we were close to arriving and Mum joked that I was like this as a baby, the minute they put me in a car, I fell asleep. I saw the school in the distance, and the lodge was on the outer grounds such that I would be able to walk to the school every day by myself. Mum was her cheerful self, oh why, oh, why couldn't I tell her the truth. I was getting angry at myself, but I was clever enough, if I had escaped once, I would find tactics to avoid them forever. I could do this. I perked up and chatted to Mum; I knew she was worried, and it was more important that I not add to her anxieties any more. I helped her unpack; we chatted and decided that I would show her around and we might even go to the nearby village if we had time the next day. The lodge was beautiful; the style reflected that of the school; it was opulent, warm and modernised. The rooms were beautifully furnished; our beds had fresh linen, which Mum was not expecting, and all my things from school had been packed, washed and ironed and returned to my bedroom. It was clear everything had been dusted, polished and cleaned in the lodge. We would find that a cleaner would come twice a week to help Mum, and she was so pleased. I wondered how Mum would pass the time when I was at school, but I need not worry, Mum was sociable and she found things to keep her busy and made friends easily.

Mum walked me to the school that first day back. She had meetings with various teachers, the nurse and this time with the headmaster. An older boy greeted me on arrival. I didn't know him, but he smiled and looked friendly. He left Mum with the nurse and took me to my first lesson. Everyone was kind that day; I still avoided the shared toilets; Mum packed me a healthy lunch; I was told that if I wanted I could have breakfast and tea at school, and some days, I loved coming early to use the library and on those days I ate the breakfast I so enjoyed at the school. I also enjoyed the lovely teas, but now I could bring lunch and always had dinner with Mum. I started to gain weight and no longer looked skeletal. I was always slim, but eventually, the gaunt look seen only in children on documentaries about starving children left me. I was happier as I wasn't hungry the whole time. I joined the debate, chess and maths club. I continued to play hockey, swam and loved cricket. There were no more incidents, and I started to relax.

Two weeks passed faster than I expected, and I ran home on Friday as we finished at 12 pm to find Mum had packed the car. She had made me lunch and a flask of chai, so as soon as I had changed out of my school uniform, we could leave for London. I gained eight kilograms in two weeks. I fitted my clothes better, even though Mum said I was getting taller each and every day and she could now buy clothes that she thought would be far too big for me, but I grew into them in the blink of an eye. As she drove us home, we chatted, sang along to pop songs, to her Hindi music CDs, and we listened to some of the old family favourite songs that we knew every word to. I neither napped nor fell asleep; I was so happy to be going home. I ate my lunch and made her share bites; she even sipped my chai. Having left early, we totally missed the Friday traffic jams to London and reached home in record time. Popa came out as soon as Mum drove the car into the drive, and I wondered how long he had been waiting for us. He took our bags, hugged us both and said he had the chai brewing for us. I was so touched when I got into the house, he had laid out the teacups, there were snacks and even homemade soup with croutons. We had a small bowl of soup, then chai with a big slice of cake. Popa had to finish some work, so Mum and I would go to collect my sisters from school. I was worried that we wouldn't have half-term holidays at the same time, but thankfully, we did. Popa had decided we would go away for four days and on Sunday we would drive to the coast. It would be too cold to swim, but no one would stop us water lovers from paddling in the sea and playing on the beach. We were all so excited.

As expected, my sisters jumped at us as if they had not seen us in months, but it had been only twelve days. Both noticed that I looked better and were not shy to tell me so; they waved goodbye to their friends; we saw one of our cousins also at the same primary school and he came to walk home with us. The older children could safely walk home on their own, but my parents liked to collect Gulshan as she was only six years old. Sometimes she begged to be allowed to come home with the older children and my parents would relent, but generally, an adult collected all the children. They had book bags, sports kits, paintings, homework and bits of craft they had made, so I helped retrieve these and carried the majority for the two sisters who skipped and chatted to each other, to us and to people who passed us on our short walk home. We did bicker, rarely, but they were such happy souls, excited by everything and questioned anything that made them curious that it was much easier to get on with them. Even at such a young age, they were confident, happy and carefree. They made everyone around them feel the same. They really exemplified what a bundle of joy meant. I had heard Popa say to Mum how he worried that they were too trusting, and I had never understood what this meant, but after what I had seen at my school, I understood. I had decided that I would teach them to be more street smart, wise and be aware without scaring them of the horrors that existed out there. When older, my two sisters really argued and disagreed, had tantrums and weeks would pass when they did not speak to each other. They were much more street smart and aware, though I still found them to be far too trusting.

We got home to find Popa's brother, our aunt and their two children were visiting with food. They stayed, and we shared the homemade pizzas, salad and finished it with apple strudel and ice cream. We played games, whilst the adults chatted. This family wasn't able to come to the coast with us at the weekend so we caught up on the gossip and would see them again on our return. More cousins popped in that night, and the telephone rang constantly. Everyone noticed how much better I looked and said how happy they were with this. They missed us, but Popa had definitely made the right decision. No one asked about future arrangements; it was clear that I was still worried and Popa was trying his best to make decisions to suit everyone, but we were all aware that things would change if we moved. The family would no longer be this close in physical distance, convenience and in terms of emotional support when we moved to Berkshire. No one wanted to think about that right now. It was inevitable and did not need to be discussed in these times of joy and our return home.

Mum was expecting to spend Saturday doing housework, but Popa had kept his word; everything was clean; he had even mowed the lawn; there was plenty of food as he had shopped, and the girls were organised and sorted. We packed for the holiday and even managed to go out to the park and walk back via Mum's family for a late lunch. My uncle loved a game called carrom; he got the board out, and we played in teams of two. It involved flicking pieces that resembled the circular pieces of draughts. Talcum powder was sprinkled to act as a lubricant on the wooden board about a metre by metre in size with pocket holes similar to those in snooker in the corner and sides in which the circular draught pieces could fit into and land in the mesh pockets. A knockout schedule was set up, and my uncle would call out names of teams to come and play, until the finale when we all gathered around the carrom board to watch and cheer the finalists. At the end of the tournament, there was chai and desserts; some of my cousins were hungry already and picked at any leftover food whilst we ate our pudding.

We got up early on Sunday; we just ate cereal, toast and tea and would have brunch when we arrived at the coast. Popa was always right, if we left early, then we missed all the traffic and instead of wasting hours sitting in the car in traffic jams caused by families travelling during half term, we had the extra hours on holiday instead. Two other families were coming; some of the kids including Remi had brought along a friend, so there were a lot of children aged six to sixteen years. We had booked three cottages in a row. Mum had started to lay the table in our cottage as we had been the first to arrive; as the other families appeared, they unpacked the luggage and came to us for eggs, fresh bread Popa had stopped to buy at the local bakery, there was toast, homemade jams, honey, biscuits and Asian snacks. Mum told us not to fill up on snacks as we were having a roast dinner later that day. We left the adults and went to investigate the beach. It was cool but not cold so we got out and carried the bucket and spades. Some of the children had even changed into and worn their swimming costumes under their coats. We collected shells, paddled, but no one took off their coats as when the wind blew, it was quite cold. We ran, found some lovely pebbles and then built a sandcastle village with a huge castle decorated with shells and beautiful stones. Popa and Mum's brother came to eventually call us back; they knew we had no idea of the time, and I noticed that the sun was starting to go down, and it was really chilly now.

We were made to shower, wash feet and change into warmer clothes. I cannot describe the smells coming out of the kitchen. It was actually my uncle who prepared the roast, each cottage had a different meat cooking and the older children had prepared and roasted or boiled the vegetables. The women had gone into the nearby town to look around. They returned and helped make gravy. All the food was laid out on the tables in the largest of the cottages for everyone to help themself. There was a lamb joint, two large chickens and a whole salmon stuffed with prawns and baked with butter oozing out, as trays of roast potatoes, vegetables and Yorkshire pudding were laid out; the meat was carved and sectioned. Steaming gravy was poured over plates laden with food. The fresh sea air and company made food taste so much better. The children sat on the floor and the adults squeezed around the two tables. I could not believe that twenty people had managed to fit so comfortably in one of the cottages. We chatted, listened to stories and ate slowly, savouring every mouthful. I had started with salmon and managed to eat a slice of lamb. There was so much food left; we would eat leftovers for lunch the next day. Desserts were various-flavoured, shop-bought cheesecakes, but I could not manage any just then. I would have two small slices of cheesecake, a white chocolate and another of strawberry, later on, in the evening.

We had decided to prepare entertainment for the next day as the forecast was for rain. We formed groups, went to the different cottages and discussed ideas or practised songs and skits. One of my cousins called Hatim and Uncle played the guitar, and I was sure we would end up singing songs. I loved these holidays. After we were bored practising, we played games, searched for movies and completed jigsaw puzzles, the radio played quietly and the adults chatted. Some of the families had returned to their own cottages, and Hatim came and asked if I wanted to go for a walk. I loved Hatim; he was like my older brother. He had fought his parents and refused to go away to private school, and I admired him anyway but so much more that he had done that. Why was I not strong enough to be like my idol? Maybe I could ask him for help to convince my parents to let me move back to London, although having Mum close and living at home at night made me feel safer, and I was starting to settle down at the new school.

Hatim and I ended up on the beach; it was cold and drizzling but still lovely. The moon was out, and it was a bright night. We just stood and watched the sea lashing to the shores, and we had to run backwards when the waters almost reached our shoes. Hatim placed his arm gently around my shoulders, and we started to walk along the shore. He asked how school was and I nodded and said, "Fine." We kept walking and he said he thought I was brave; he would have hated to leave his family and go away, no matter how much our grandfather wanted it. Hatim said sometimes we just had to be strong and fight for what we thought was right, and I nodded in agreement. He didn't speak for a while. Then, he bluntly asked me if anything terrible had happened. I turned and faced him and then I couldn't stop talking. I told him about the food being taken, the older boys abusing the younger ones and that it had almost happened to me. He gave me a hug and held me tightly. I hadn't realised that tears had streamed down my face. Hatim took a handkerchief out of his pocket and wiped my face; I found a tissue in my pocket and blew my nose. Hatim told me not to worry; he started to talk about the songs he was thinking of playing in tomorrow's entertainment show, and we never talked about what I had shared with him ever again.

Monday was fabulous; we stole or rather helped ourselves to our parents' clothes to make costumes. Breakfast and lunch were a help-yourself affair as everyone was busy either being made to sew, paint cardboard or copy lines onto cards. All the food left over from the day before was demolished. The room was decorated, and we all squeezed into the largest cottage where we had all spent a lot of time already. There were skits, songs, some bad magic tricks, songs, poems and a play of the children pretending to be their parents, which made me laugh so much my sides hurt, even though I was playing Popa and he pretended to look sternly at me as if offended, but I saw his eyes beaming with happiness at my imitation voice of him. My favourite was seeing my cousins do a lovely Indian dance; we hadn't seen them practising so it was a lovely surprise; my eldest girl cousin had roped the six youngest to do a form of Bharat Natyam dance, enacted a part of the Hindu religious stories, but it was so cute, and they got all their moves correct after only a few practices. As expected, when Hatim played the songs we all knew so well, everyone joined in and we sang a few English and Hindi songs.

One of my uncles' families was leaving early the next morning so that night we had booked to go to a fish and chips shop; it was a popular take away shop, but they had seating in the back, and as it was Monday, cold, wet and off-season, we managed to get a booking for everyone. They had lined two long tables with chairs for us. We all loved the meal; some of the women just had fish and salad but even they stole a few chips. The fish was so fresh, with crispy yellow batter and so large, the younger children shared one piece and struggled to finish it. We were allowed to drink Coca Cola as a treat because it went so well with fried food. The man said he could make deep-fried Mars bars if we wanted, but we were so full and actually it sounded so disgusting, this indulgence was refused.

We left midday on Wednesday back to London as Popa had to work, and even Mum said she had a few chores to do. The week passed much too quickly; we visited cousins when our parents were busy and soon it was Sunday and time to pack and go back to Berkshire to my private school and the lodge with Mum. I had raised the idea of staying in London a few times, but it went nowhere, and Popa cut that discussion short before it started. He reminded me that I was not to worry and they, as parents, knew what they were doing. He said he was coming with us and staying for a week but did not say why. Had Hatim said anything to him? I asked Hatim, but he said that I was not to worry about anything. My sisters would stay with their aunt for a week and Popa would return the following weekend. I hated having to say goodbye to everyone, to my sisters and to London. I hadn't made a single close friend at school; I nodded to a few boys in my class; my old roommates said hello and always asked how I was or stopped to share a few words, but none were closer than that to me. At school, I felt lonely; I tried to pretend it did not matter, but a week in London reminded me how nice it is to have someone to share gossip and general life with.

We left London Sunday afternoon; I managed to doze in the car, and it seemed like I had just shut my eyes and we were already at the lodge. As before it had been cleaned, there was milk in the fridge even though my parents had stopped and shopped, the bedrooms had fresh bedding, towels in the bathrooms were washed and the whole place smelled clean and fresh. Mum made cheese toasties with soup, and I went upstairs to check I had completed all my homework and was prepared for the next day. I put on my pyjamas after showering and had got into bed to read, but when Mum came upstairs to check on me, she found me fast asleep. She took my book from my hand, tucked me in and turned off the lights. It had been a busy and fun week, and it had tired me out. Also, she knew I was nervous about going back to school the next day and was relieved to see me fast asleep.

Both my parents walked me to school, but they did not come inside, and I felt a huge relief. I wondered why Popa had come. I found out a few days later. He and Mum went to visit the local primary schools and found one to enrol my sisters. They also looked at a few houses to rent, but Popa actually found one he could actually afford to buy. It was much smaller than our beautiful home in London but easily affordable, and the girls would have to share a bedroom, but it would be ours. It had a small garden and was walking distance from all our schools. My parents would find a bigger home later on, but at the moment, they wanted to keep the London home and could not afford anything bigger. I was just relieved to hear that I would continue to be a day boarder and I could cope with that. I still thought my parents were making a mistake and we should have returned to London as soon as a school could be found for me, but I knew there were times when it did me no good to argue with my parents.

School was bearable. I had been bumped into and punched a few times when the older boys who had tried to abuse me found that they could get away with it. Once, the nice prefect who had collected me that day I returned to school with Mum saw them, and he intervened and warned them off. I learned quickly to never be alone and hung around where there were gangs of boys my age or in communal areas. I always stayed where I knew there were kinder prefects or teachers. Popa had come into the school and met my form tutor and the housemaster; they were all keeping an eye on me, and although they were not happy with my quietness, I had at least gained weight, joined a few clubs and now participated in general school life. I had been asked to submit a story for English, and it was so good it had been entered into a county-wide competition, and I had been selected into the final five shortlist to win a prize of five thousand pounds for my school and the winning prize was a two-day training at RADA in London. I actually won that competition. One of the older boys had interviewed me for the school newspaper, took my photo and wrote an article, which had pleased everyone. I even won the English prize for my year at the end of the academic school year, which again added to the pride felt by my parents and family.

As I was leaving the chess club and about to walk across the school grounds to the lodge, two older boys came to talk to me. I instinctively felt scared. They asked me if I wanted to join a special club, I would be introduced as a new member and would have to be initiated by doing a few dares. They said that it was useful to have friends and contacts; they could help me go far in life. I had the look, wealth and success already an indication from the English competition that showed them I would go far in life and my results from homework showed I was highly intelligent and competent. This stood me well in such a school. I didn't reply, and they told me to take a few days to think about it then give them an answer on the following Monday. I breathed a long sigh of relief when they left without harming me, and I was so glad that they were not the abusers or bullies I had anticipated. I went home and told my parents about what they had said. My parents then told me that Hatim had told them what had happened, they had spoken to the teachers and didn't I want the boys punished? I shook my head. They told me not to be scared, but I lied that I did not see the boys again and was not sure I would be able to identify them. I changed the conversation and asked them, instead, what I should do about what the boys offered me that day. Popa advised me to be friendly and polite, but any club that involved initiation sounded dodgy so I should keep my distance.

When the two boys came to me again to ask what I had decided, I told them what had happened to me in my first half-term. They said they knew such things happened; the school was trying to stop it, but it was hard to stop as no one complained. They promised to keep an eye on me and the younger pupils, even though I said that I was not ready to join any exclusive clubs. They were so reasonable, I hoped they would keep their word and look after the younger boys and not hold it against me that I had not accepted their offer. This was exactly what happened. I never had any more problems from any of the older boys ever again.

In the second year, I continued to gain weight, was taller and towered above my classmates. I started to use communal bathrooms and went to all parts of the school as I wanted to see what was happening there. I still noticed that some of the younger boys were getting bullied; it was more covert and so the older boys and prefects could not stop it. If I could, I would intervene whenever possible. I had become more confident, had actually made friends, but the injustice and the thought of the fear I had felt when I started at the school made me want to stop other young boys feeling such hurt. I had heard that even some of the older boys experienced bullying and abuse. I never forgot that there had been two attempted suicides and we needed to talk, be open and raise alarms about any abuse. The school had a school council where pupils met teachers to discuss and resolve issues, but only the older boys were invited to join. I started a campaign that there should be representatives from the lower school; I petitioned younger pupils to sign up if they agree with me, got many signatures, even from older pupils and the deputy headmaster called me into his office to discuss my ideas. The school changed its policies and said that the six pupils for the school council could come from any year and there would be no age limit, and when we had elections, I stood and won a seat in the school council.

At the first meeting and throughout my time at my school, I discussed why I had wanted things to change. I was open in discussing what had happened to me; I knew what happened to younger pupils and I believed that it also happened to older pupils. We had had two more attempts at suicide that year, luckily both boys were all right but were offered as much support as they needed, and I knew the school was concerned and wanted such things to change. The teachers were aware, but in all these years, they had never managed to change or totally stop bullying and abuse. I had many ideas; we needed CCTV in certain areas, instead of mentors there should be a buddy system and punishment for offenders should be more severe including expulsion of perpetrators. Articles were published in the school paper, and once a school culture is open and transparent, change starts to happen. Of course, I was not stupid enough to think that change would be immediate and forever, but if it reduced pain felt by one boy and stopped e.g. suicide, I knew it was worth it.

My parents were worried that all this extra work would impact on my grades and make perpetrators attack me, but actually, it helped me build confidence, developed survival tactics and I now knew to surround myself with friends and supporters that gave me some protection. Also it helped being so tall and eating mum's food made me strong and healthy. I was never bullied at that school again. A lot of change happened; there were now more day boarders, young pupils were buddied into support pairs, older pupils were not allowed in younger boys rooms and house masters had rooms next door to the dormitories of the youngest children. Two counsellors were hired and all pupils had access to them without having to give detailed accounts of why they needed support. Teachers were more supportive; they knew hidden areas of the school that needed to be patrolled, and there was better overall care of all the boys who attended this school.

I stopped asking my parents to move back to London, but none of my cousins were forced to go to private school unless it was something they wanted after Hatim had quietly told all the adults in our family what kinds of things happen to children in private school. He never named me as having suffered, but I wouldn't have minded now if he had as I no longer felt shame.

Popa left on Sunday morning; he returned with the girls the following weekend to show them their new school, and we all visited the new house they had placed an offer on. It was so small compared to our London home, but we did not complain as long as we were together. I also showed them my school; they all came to watch me play in the school hockey team against a local school and cheered when we won. Popa took us to Nandos on Saturday night to celebrate the match win and told my sisters about my English story competition, and they begged me to read it to them later that night. I had stopped feeling bad about how all our lives were changing because of me, we were only two hours maximum drive from the wider family, and although we could no longer pop in and see the family, at least we five would be our tight little family, and I knew that would help me in the long term. I stopped feeling guilty and accepted my parents' decision; they really did know what they were doing.

Chapter 7
Love and Life!

We had so much fun at the wedding reception; we ate; we danced, and I am sure we managed to chat to every guest, eventually, or at least dance with them. Fiona, Tim's wife, came with their two-year-old daughter to have a dance with us, and we discovered she was pregnant again. We knew there were a few Muslim families' friends and members of the community who did not approve of dancing or having any anglicised traditions in the Muslim wedding, but we tried to make everyone happy, and to be honest, we wanted us to be happy. Tasneem's father was one of them, but his son had eventually got his parents up to dance, and they did a kind of Bhangra dance when they saw that no one was judging them and a few of their equally devout friends had got up to stand, moved side to side and join in with the dancing or they clapped and watched when we danced. Usually, the bride and groom leave, but Tasneem asked if we could stay when the elders left, and I was happy to do so as I did not want to leave either. We had the rest of our lives together, but I knew this would be our one and only wedding. We had nowhere to rush to, and I knew I had the rest of the weekend with only her so I was happy to stay and carry on with the celebrations. They put on western pop music, and we danced to all our old favourite dance music and even ended with a couple of slow dances where there was no embarrassment as other couples joined us and friends swayed in circles chatting, smiling and unconcerned by the romance in the room. I took Tasneem and kissed her, something I would never have done in front of her parents. It is so hard to meet other people romantically within our communities in these days of internet dating and social media, and we enjoyed watching the young people chatting and flirting. Some were obviously shy, girls danced with friends and the boys tried to impress the girls with imitation of Michael Jackson or Bollywood dancing. It was a wonderful, fun and relaxed night.

We actually ended up getting kicked out of our venue, but there was no rudeness or nastiness. The manager came and said they needed to start to clear up and the staff needed to go home as they had another wedding the next day and needed to return early to get the place ready. We thanked them, gave the staff a generous tip and left. There were a few family cars left, and Tasneem said we should all go back to the flat and continue the party. The others laughed and said they would drive us home, but were not staying and Tasneem frowned although I could see even, she was getting tired, having worn high heels all day.

Tasneem was cradled in my arms in the back of the seat in the car on our way home. Remi and her husband chatted to us as they drove us, but we weren't really listening. I couldn't wait to spend a second night with my beautiful, intelligent and sexy wife. The best was yet to come. Tasneem suddenly sat up and she reminded me of a meerkat I saw on some television advert; she asked her sister-in-law where they were going as this was not the way to our flat. She looked behind and the other cars were still following. She was worried and asked where we were going. I told her they were taking her to a secret wedding gift that I had arranged for her, and she saw that I was excited, but I could tell she was anxious that I would be upset if she did not like it. I think she assumed we were going to another hotel.

I had always let her choose what she wanted when we needed to buy each other gifts; we were very relaxed with each other about such things. We were easily pleased with gifts of food, but when it came to the big and important presents, we always shopped together. We often had ideas of what we wanted to get each other, but the final choice was always made jointly, with honesty about it being what the other one liked, so we never got upset or had to pretend to like something we clearly did not like. Everything with Tasneem was temperate; she rarely complained, was open in telling me if she liked something or not and hated me spending too much on her, and this was our only point of conflict and contention. She always called anything expensive a waste of money and would always want to buy something cheaper. I stood my ground; quality always lasts longer. She was adventurous and never refused, always tried new things like food; we visited so many places in London and some she didn't enjoy, but she always attempted it all. She made me take her to see an opera and struggled to stay awake but would not let us leave early as she insisted, she had to get her money's worth so we watched the whole thing, and we left with her having tears in her eyes, as it had moved her so much when we got to the end.

I really did not want the flat to be our home where we started our married life together. This has given me sleepless nights. Mimi had ruined it and so I had rented it out a week ago and moved into our new house without telling Tasneem.

I had talked to my parents and sisters one weekend after the engagement and when Tasneem was away visiting her aunt with her parents. My family knew about everything Mimi had done to me, and I had been thinking of selling and moving before I met Tasneem, but I had never made the time to look for somewhere else. I spent most weekends away, just sleeping at the flat during the week. I had been embarrassed to take Tasneem there, and she said we would redecorate and it would be fine, but I had bad memories now of how it had been with Mimi and the horrors she had left behind. Remi and Gulshan totally understood how I felt; they helped me search for a new home for Tasneem and me and managed to find a new-build in a lovely eco-friendly development ten minutes from the hospital. It was near completion so we, my family, all met and we went to see it. Every house had solar panels, water was recycled and the materials used were as sustainable as possible and the house itself met some special merit award for reflecting the German model of modern eco-build. I loved it immediately and was sure Tasneem would feel the same. My parents came down and stayed with me so we could go to see the house. I also asked Tasneem's father for his advice; he came to see it, and we all liked the property straight away. It was a large townhouse, had four bedrooms and a reasonable garden, and we could decide on the final fittings to suit our needs. My family was nervous about not telling Tasneem, but her father agreed with me and said she would love it. My worry was not involving her in decisions about the fittings, but I would let her decorate and furnish it in any way she wanted. I put down a deposit that day as the remaining properties were selling fast. I spent the next few months emailing designs for the interior and chose a modern, high end fitted kitchen with lots of cupboard space that I knew Tasneem would absolutely love. I wasn't totally stupid or inconsiderate; one weekend I had taken her shopping and asked her to go into an interior designer to look at ideas of how our future home could be designed and furnished, and asked if there was anything particular she liked for the flat. That had been so much fun, we spent about three hours looking and discussing her favourites; and I made sure I noted it all. If only she knew that what she was suggesting was actually what would go into our new home, and I was so happy I had done this as she chose some things, colours and had preferences for our home I would never have thought of.

I promised my family I knew what I was doing, had covertly got ideas from Tasneem and if there was anything she didn't like, I would change it, but I was only getting the basics for now. What I ordered was the kitchen that I had actually shown Tasneem and she had loved, with the large stove, a double oven, fridge freezer, washing machine and dishwasher. I knew the make and model she liked. I bought a double bed, some Italian dining room furniture, new bedding, towels and one sofa. There was a whole house that Tasneem and I could shop to furnish later. I knew she would enjoy helping to design the garden so I did nothing to that, except taking what came with the house, a patio and a bit of lawn. It had been so hard to hide all my arrangements from Tasneem; there were so many times when I almost let it slip because I was so excited, but she was so busy with wedding arrangements that she did not see me squirm a few times.

We had a double garage, and I had left my car in one garage; the others parked outside. Tasneem asked what this was and I asked my sister Remi to give Tasneem the box I had asked her to look after in her handbag. We got out of the car and the others all surrounded us and I asked her to open the box. It contained her house keys. I told her I had bought this house for her, our new home, and I was shaking either from the cool night or the fear that she would hate it. My mum and sisters had planted roses that would flower in the summer, lots of plants and pots containing plants and flowers lined the front of the house. She walked to look at them and bent to smell the flowers. It was 1 am, but she was in no hurry to open the door. We all stood in suspense, and Tasneem was oblivious to all this; I think it was all just sinking in that this was to be our new home. Her brother could stand it no longer; he came up to her, took the keys from her hand and opened the front door as I lifted her in my arms and did the British tradition of carrying her over the threshold. She smiled and laughed; the others clapped, then followed us in and demanded tea. My sisters laughed and asked everyone to say good night and leave. They were dying to see Tasneem's reaction to our new home, but they left and promised to come with food late the next afternoon.

It was late, and we were all tired. Tasneem wouldn't let me pull her up to the bedroom. Instead she kicked off her heels and before I could take my shoes off, she ran and went to the kitchen first as I knew she would. She said it was huge, recognised the kitchen we had seen a while ago, realised what I had done and smiled. She opened drawers and doors, found the fridge that was stocked with breakfast and lots more; she even looked inside the oven, washing machine and dishwasher. Then she went to the pantry, checked the downstairs bathroom and peeked into the dining room and two sitting rooms. She loved the Italian dining room furniture and asked why the sitting rooms were so empty except for the one sofa? I frowned and pretended to be tired and started to go upstairs, and she ran to me and kissed me. We walked upstairs together. She kept a flowing dialogue of questions, astonished by every part of the house, looking at me and then getting distracted by a fixture or a colour I had chosen. It hadn't been the sterile white of the flat; I had a few feature walls with colour and wallpaper. She even looked in one room and thought how much our future children would love this room!

She had a quick look at the other bedrooms but threw herself on our bed. No one, but she and I would ever sleep in that bed. Well, I was wrong about that, my sons joined us any chance they got! She said she loved the house and loved me. She wanted to know when and how I had managed to buy a house without her knowing a thing. I kissed her to stop her talking, but she pulled away and was going to start her questions and there was only one way to stop that. I helped her get out of her clothes, and as always, she wanted to wash before we made love.

I had told both our extended families about the house and they had come to see it the previous weeks, and like her father approved of the choice, commenting on the parking, every aspect of the inside, the garden and how close it was to the hospital. Tasneem's sister Tara had arranged some of her new clothes in the bedroom wardrobes and drawers so that there were no suitcases to unpack that night. Tasneem came back wearing a beautiful white cotton and lace nightie; I had showered in the family bathroom and lay naked in bed waiting for her. She was still shy and a little shocked that I was naked, and she took her time getting in bed with me. I let her take as much time as she needed; we kissed and touched each other. I needed nothing to get me aroused; I absolutely loved her and liked her gentle pace. I loved learning together, and we spent a long time investigating, whispering and getting to know each other's body. I asked her if what I was doing was okay with her, and she just nodded or kissed me back to demonstrate her approval. We were in no rush about anything. She often fell asleep during foreplay as she led such a busy life, even after marriage she often visited her parents; she would return with food, still did all her father's accounts and still paid for their home. She had been afraid to tell me how much they relied on her, but I knew all this. She had been so honest, and I needed nothing from her, though I don't think she ever let me pay for all the food she bought for us, even though I had insisted on a joint account so we never needed to be embarrassed to ask for, query or worry about money and how it was spent. When my family or friends visited, we were hospitable and as generous as family and friends had been to us. We trusted and loved each other. For me being in love was not about sex, it was about the closeness of someone who loved you simply just by lying next to you. I never struggled to fall asleep and never felt unsafe, as long as Tasneem was near or next to me.

As promised, both families came the next day, before even waiting for us to speak, everyone questioned and wanted to know what Tasneem thought about the house, and she pretended to be angry, but it fooled no one. Her joy was abundantly visible to all who saw her face; her eyes were a catalyst to her smile; she wanted to show everyone our very empty home and couldn't believe they had all already seen the house. The empty rooms were ideal for us to share food that first day; we ate as is traditionally done in many Muslim cultures; we set picnic-like sections on the floor using table cloths and plastic to cover the new carpet, food came piping hot and so it was taken into the kitchen to be served, some was placed in the oven to keep warm and there was a flurry of activity. Everyone seemed to know what to do without being instructed. Even the children were set tasks; there was an assembly set up between the kitchen and the dining areas. There was chatter; one of the children had put music on their phone and the two sets of parents sat on the dining table watching all the action.

We hadn't gotten out of bed until past midday. After making us a drink, I snuck in with Tasneem into her shower to her horror, but she relaxed when I kissed her back. I soaped and scrubbed it. I loved touching her body. She told me to stop, else she would never get ready in time for everyone visiting. I had to let her go and showered as she dressed. She had made the beds and hung our wedding clothes to air them. I got dressed, and she had already put croissants to warm in the oven and was cutting up a mango to go with a bowl of strawberries, grapes and muesli. We had very similar tastes in food, although I seemed to eat twice as much as her. The chai was bubbling in a pot, so I strained the tea leaves and poured the tea into two large mugs. I had gotten her to stop taking sugar, but occasionally, she liked to have a little sugar, but she told me not today, she would have jam with her croissant instead. As we ate breakfast, she suddenly saw the garden. I had to tell her to finish her breakfast before she ran into the garden. She was so childlike when it came to excitement and new experiences. We only had the shoes we wore to the wedding, and I could see she was thinking how she could go into the garden, her heels would not survive the soft lawn, and she had to be satisfied with looking out from the porch until she unpacked some flip flops and her gardening shoes. We only just managed to clear away breakfast and the families started to arrive.

It was a mad and chaotic, spontaneous housewarming party. Family came with more presents, a coffee machine was unpacked, set-up and the smells of freshly made coffee was wonderful, especially when cinnamon had been added to the brewing beans. Tara had to go and find some shoes Tasneem could wear into the garden as she was already discussing her plans to plant flowers and seeds interspersed with vegetables and herbs. She wanted dwarf fruit trees and fruit-bearing bushes. She told her brother that she would leave him a list of jobs when we went on our honeymoon. Tasneem's father had arrived with an ice cream cake that fitted easily into our almost empty freezer, and we watched him slice it up and plates were passed to all our guests, about fifty of them when it was time for dessert. Tim and Fiona came later on in the afternoon to say goodbye before they flew back to their home in Scotland, and we already pencilled in a time when we would visit them in two months' time. Their child had made friends with children in our family and went upstairs to play with a samosa in their hand. They said they were still full from all the food from the wedding, but Tim and Fiona managed to finish the food on their plate given to them. If Mum could have, she would have packed them food to take back to Scotland, but they had flown with one of the budget airlines and most of their hand luggage had contained things for their daughter. I think Mum still managed to pack them a few snacks for the journey, but she listened to their protestations about needing no more cooked food that day.

Only about half of the homes in the new development had people moved in and that was useful as our guests all stayed, making noise that no one could complain about. People came and went all day, and it amazed me how the food never ran out. An empty house was ideal, children played hide and seek or made-up games. I hadn't unpacked the television as I wasn't sure which sitting room to use and Tasneem had conversations with various people about which would be best. She wondered if she could fit in a visit to the shops tomorrow to buy more furniture, and we just managed to convince her that there was no rush; our families did not complain about sitting on the floor on the thick carpet for now. What was lovely was that our home fit all our families easily, and there was a lovely snapshot of all the parties and meals we would have with family and friends in the future. We were happy to have everyone stay, but as the night got cold, we were reminded that some people had work and school to go to on the next day, and our families started to leave. We were sad, we loved having everyone come and visit in our new home.

No one bothered us on Monday. The house had been left clean and tidy. Tasneem and I had another leisurely morning, most of it spent in bed, and today, we had nothing to rush for. Breakfast was more like lunch; we kept trying to get up, but one or both of us got distracted! We finally got up properly, bathed, ate, dressed and then we walked around the development so I could show her around. There were still some building and refurbishments happening; we saw workmen and waved to the few people we met who had moved in. At one end, there were some flats, a gym and a coffee shop. We found that there were paths constructed and shortcuts to the nearby high street. One bedroom was full of boxes and suitcases that needed to be unpacked, but we decided to leave all this for another day. Instead, we packed and got ready for the honeymoon.

The choice and the full arrangements of the honeymoon was Tasneem's idea, and we would leave in two days' time. She chose for us to spend ten days in Malaysia, one week for us and a few days visiting Umayma and her family. I hadn't realised that Tasneem followed certain Islamic traditions, so I had never seen her legs bare until we married; she always covered them with trousers, long skirts and jeans or the work scrubs, but I had never thought about it. She had only gone swimming in a women's only pool; she had never worn a traditional swimming costume in public; the one she had almost covered her entire body and she had not remembered to bring one for Malaysia even though she was desperate to be by the sea. By now, I had seen every part of her, and I could not understand why she was still so shy. I had brought along two sets of snorkelling equipment and told her to wear leggings and a tee-shirt, and it didn't matter that she didn't have a swimming costume, but I wanted to teach her how to snorkel. She of course loved it, and we even managed to buy her a swimming costume that she liked later that week. It had a long skirt and wasn't at all revealing so she did not need to feel shy when she was swimming in public. The beaches in Malaysia had a mixture of tourists; most were either Muslims or aware of the Islamic culture and even the most liberal person knew to cover up, and there were none of the almost semi-naked bodies one sees throughout Europe. Malaysia is quite liberal, but guidebooks advise being respectful and this was seen throughout. Local people were as covered as Tasneem when swimming; the sea was full of men, women, young people and children. Some were bathing fully dressed in their everyday cotton clothes, heads covered and men wore shorts or trousers, but we never saw women in bikinis. Malaysia has clean, warm beaches, clear, warm seas, and we chose to stay about an hour from Narathiwat, where Umayma's family lived. The water mirrored the sky and the waters were transparent as much effort was made to stop sewage effluent entering these waters. We did not have to search far to find tropical fishes; there were calm inlets that had a kaleidoscope of colours. I showed Tasneem the few dangerous spiky sea urchins to avoid, and we did not see any jellyfish, much to my relief, but I had shown her how they looked and warned her against swimming anywhere near or touching them. In fact, I told her to try not to touch anything, just in case!

Umayma's family were overjoyed when we called and told them we were coming to visit them whilst on our honeymoon. She came with her grandparents, parents, uncle and aunt and her two younger siblings to our hotel on day two. We had to insist they stayed and had lunch with us. We had booked to stay in a beachfront chalet where we had our own chef and people who came to clean brought us breakfast and looked after us throughout our stay. Our chef was not at all fazed by our guests, and in fact, he admired us for knowing his people. He cooked a huge fish, rice, vegetables and a spicy sauce. One of the staff brought over another table, plates and glasses. Drinks of fresh juices and soda water were also brought, and we sat under shade, ate as we watched the sea, and then we all went and had a paddle. They initially kept saying they were leaving, but once we ate, they were less formal and relaxed. We walked and talked; Umayma and her two brothers were splashing and collecting shells and pebbles. They would run up to us to show us what they had found, give Tasneem their best finds and then run back into the sea with their trousers hiked up to the knees but still managed to get soaked. We went back to our chalet, had dessert and more drinks, and then we walked with them to the bus stop. In Malaysia, if you see a bus and wave your arm, they stop to let you board. Everyone piled into a minibus that looked quite full, but somehow, all our guests fitted in and off they went to a lot of waving and words were shouted that we had no understanding of as by now they were far away. Umayma had kept up her English, and her uncle and aunt spoke it sufficiently well so we had conversed through them. They spoke basic English due to tourism, but we managed to communicate easily. The grandparents had sat close to us, constantly smiled, nodded, touched and patted our hands as conversations were translated. It had been a wonderful day.

They invited us to spend an afternoon with them. We hired a driver and explored as much of that side of the country as we could. Malaysia and its people are truly welcoming, warm, generous and hospitable. We met Umayma's close family, friends and a huge extended family. They hugged and squeezed Tasneem and kissed her forehead like they do with Muslims who have returned from performing the Hajj or pilgrimage to Mecca. She was their celebrity and saviour. They were polite with me; all kissed the back of my hand and many of the older women touched my cheek, lovingly. A simple feast fed every visitor, family and neighbours who had helped to set tables as had been done for us at the beach.

Young people served food to the elderly women and men; we had learned to eat every little serving and slowly as more would be piled onto our plate the minute we finished. Tasneem and I were sitting far from each other, and we had people translating. They spoke so quickly, I am sure we missed much of what was said, but it did not matter, there was joy and happy conversations, and it was easy to follow conversations about the everyday lives of these lovely people. Tasneem and I would look at each other and smile; this made the women giggle and whisper words to each other that no one bothered to translate. Photos were taken and we sat and ate for a few hours whilst watching the children play, people talk and the world around us passing by in joyous waves.

Umayma's father and uncle had arranged to come to visit us again; they took us out to sea in a boat; we fished; we caught nothing, but they caught two different fish, which they cleaned and cooked for us even though our chef was happy to do the cooking. This was their treat. They would tug at our arms and point to various sights they wanted to show us. We were invited again on the Friday as Malaysia is a Muslim country and Jummah is a big deal and a holiday. We arrived for prayers on Friday and then went to join the other families for a late lunch cooked at the mosque. We were introduced to so many more people and then taken back to their home for tea and desserts. Umayma's mum had made a Malaysian outfit for Tasneem; she had crocheted all the edges herself with fine silk thread, and it was stunning. On the last visit to their home, Tasneem dressed in it, and it suited her. She did her hair and make-up especially to go with the outfit, she looked lovely, and I could see how touched they were when they saw her in it. Tasneem gave them presents on the last day as she thought that if she gave them at the start, they would feel obliged to inundate us in return. Most of our one large luggage was full of presents that Tasneem and my mum had bought for Umayma and her family. Of course, Umayma's mum had done the same; there were presents for us to take back, beautifully carved wood, shawls, table cloths and Muslim head scarves for all of our families, for some doctors and nurses at the hospital and of course for my parents. We were so touched. They cried as we were leaving; Umayma's mum called Tasneem Umayma's second mother; she had given birth to her and Tasneem had given her life beyond her childhood. Umayma continued to learn English and her older cousins were good at using the mobile phone and we managed to stay in touch using social media as a communication tool. We got updates and video calls from Umayma most months throughout our lives.

Tasneem got pregnant within the first year after we married; she did not want to wait and I did not mind. We had decided to visit Iran as I had promised Mum that I would take her. Tasneem was also desperate to go as well, as the two women had shared so many stories of my mum's childhood and I had told her about our previous visits. So eight months after returning from our honeymoon, we invited my parents to Iran to visit family and have a holiday. We let my mum plan the itinerary as really we were going for her benefit, but we insisted it was to be our treat for all the kindness they had bestowed on us and especially in welcoming Tasneem so easily into the family. It was during this holiday that Tasneem announced her pregnancy to all of us. She couldn't keep it a secret because she had been so sick and nauseous; we were starting to worry, and Mum was wondering if she was indeed expecting a baby. Even I had wondered. My mum managed to plan a traditional Iranian party that would be held for a pregnant woman while we were in Iran, and we had video calls from my sisters announcing their jealousy and disappointment in jest at not being invited. As is typical with both our families, mine were ecstatic and Tasneem's were overly worried.

Iran had changed, in many ways it had become quite westernised in the way the cities had expanded and grown, but in terms of values, everyone complained about politics and the restrictive rules and fear from the harassing police. We were dutiful in following exactly what was required; we dressed traditionally, women covered their heads and yet when we were within the family or with close friends, it was no different to being in London. Teenagers dressed the same, liked similar music, and of course we feasted, chatted, danced and shared a lot of laughter. It is a country full of contrast and contradictions with the effect being greatest and negative for the poorest. In many ways, more backward than countries like Malaysia, though we found Malaysia to be far more open and friendly than we anticipated. In Iran, we were warned to never discuss anything personal or political in public; we did not stay and spend much time in the city and instead, Mum planned most of our time to be in her countryside family home and other towns or villages. Here it was more relaxed and felt much less as if we were being watched the whole time. Even then we were careful as we did not want to endanger family and friends. There was a feeling of spies being everywhere.

We spent two days in Iraq on our way back home. Tasneem and I differ in the type of Muslims we are. I am very relaxed anyway when it comes to anything to do with religion, but we had some fundamental differences in beliefs that arose out of our different historical Islamic origins. She was keen to visit Iraq, which was even more oppressive, especially for women, than Iran. Iraq is a country stuck in the 1970s; we saw signs of rebuilding but also the remnants of all the wars; the poverty experienced by many was in stark contrast to the large investments into the ornate and gold-painted religious buildings, mausoleums and mosques. Tasneem and Mum knew what both countries would be like in terms of the needy and poverty so we had packed such that we had decided that we would give away as much of the luggage as we could. Tasneem went through our wardrobes and packed all the clothes we wore the least; she had asked family and friends for any clothes that were in good condition, but that could be donated and so we had two suitcases each, packed fully with clothes, toys, treats and anything that would be useful to give away. When we did a pilgrimage to a ruined old city, there were very poor people begging outside the mosque we had decided to visit and pray in. As Tasneem carried things to donate, she took out a pair of Remi's children's shoes that they had worn once or twice and grown out of so they were almost new. She went to give a pair of shoes to one child and two different children grabbed a shoe each. Neither would relent and let the other have the shoe, so in the end we had to buy another pair, get one child to give up a shoe and give each child a pair of shoes.

Tasneem's mum, of course, planned the traditional seven-month Sitabi, which is similar to the American baby shower a few months after our return and of course my sisters were very much a part of that. As with her wedding, Tasneem's hands were painted in traditional mehndi henna patterns, food was cooked and women and girls were invited to feast and spoil Tasneem. I really wanted to attend, but there is a strict no men policy and I felt left out. Pregnancy is very much about women and babies in both the Asian and Islamic world.

Tasneem had a terrible pregnancy; she was sick throughout, struggling to keep food down and after her Sitabi, she was advised to do bed rest. As a surgeon, our bodies amazed and fascinated me. Pregnancy baffled me, surely, a woman needed food and water to help their baby develop and grow healthily, the mother needed the energy to be well for the new being they were carrying as well as for themselves so why was she so nauseous? Why was nature so cruel to women? She was rarely ill. I sometimes think that when you work in a hospital your body becomes accustomed to, exposed to and produces antibodies against all kinds of germs. Tasneem couldn't ever have kept her pregnancy a secret. She started to experience severe and violent morning sickness at the start of her pregnancy, and it continued until the babies were born. Often sights and smells would make her run to the toilet; travelling could only happen if she ate no breakfast, even then she had to carry sick bags, and even though she was hungry all the time, she was unable to eat most food now. Her favourite food these days was a sugar-rich drink and salty crisps or crackers. She didn't even like ginger biscuits which everyone told her to eat, and chai now made her gag.

She always complained about the lack of research and studies done on women; in her work she found a disparity in the way women and their illnesses and medical complaints were dealt with compared to those of men. Tasneem's first midwife was terrible. She was negative and complained to Tasneem that she was thin during pregnancy because she worked too hard and didn't look after herself. The reality was that Tasneem was surrounded by women and a community who did nothing but worry about her, looked after her, supported her and she had to do nothing. Our home was cleaned, food was cooked and most of the chores were done for us. Tasneem had slackened her pace at work; she had to as she was often so tired; she was not at all silly, her baby was her priority now, but she liked to work and was aware of her limitations. The midwife did not listen but scolded her so Tasneem dismissed the appointed woman and found her own midwife who was kinder and supportive. Both of our mothers, sisters and cousins worried about Tasneem's relentless nausea. They tried every concoction to stop the vomiting; and they cooked everything to help the mother and baby develop healthily. We discovered that Tasneem's mum had also struggled during her three pregnancies, and eventually, Tasneem decided to give up work just after her Sitabi as she felt absolutely exhausted. This did not stop or abate the nausea, but at least, she could nap and be spoiled with gentle massages. Tasneem's mum wanted her to move back home, but their home was small and Tasneem preferred to stay at home, so we got used to our families and her friends often visiting and no one minded; I was relieved she was so well looked after. It was a joyous time, though I felt redundant and instead was teased constantly about this.

Ismail was born ten weeks early so it was good Tasneem had given up work and hardly had time to enjoy her maternity leave. Tasneem was relaxed and unconcerned, but I thought I would lose my mind with worry. Her sister Tara had come to stay; she was now married and lived too far to visit and go home on the same day, so she loved to come and stay with us and then with her parents for a few days. Tasneem was feeling lonely if no one visited and had asked Tara to come as my work was very busy. I had suggested we go out for a meal as we hadn't been out in ages, but Tasneem still had a difficult time with food, and I had noticed she hadn't been too unwell over the last few days. Now I realise that it was her body saving and amassing every ounce of energy it could for the pending birth. Tasneem hadn't had cravings, but the last two days she wanted dessert and asked Tara to bring a cake. When Remi visited, she was asked to bring one of the vermicelli desserts she was famous for making with almonds and cream. When I came home, I found Tara massaging Tasneem's feet and Remi rubbing her back whilst she ate a bowl of dessert. It reminded me of the day after the Nikaah. I was starving and seeing Tasneem eating dessert made me think the women had eaten earlier, but they hadn't. We set the table and I saw Tasneem was struggling more than normally. She said we should eat later as she had filled up on the cake first with Tara and then on Remi's dessert. She sat and watched us; she wanted to fuss around us, but her body stopped her, and she could barely get up and stand. Her feet hurt; despite the massage, they were swollen and I tried not to worry. Tasneem didn't eat any more that evening, but she did not throw up the desserts either to hers and my relief.

We said goodnight to both our sisters, Remi would drop Tara to her parents even though Tasneem begged her to stay and Tara said she would visit her early with their mum the next day. As we were standing outside, Tasneem placed her arm on mine and I helped her into the house. It was such a nice night; I wished we could have gone for a short walk, but I saw that Tasneem looked tired. She mocked me and wondered how she could get that exhausted just sitting around all day or having short naps. I thought she would go to bed and lie down, but she was restless and decided to have a bath, something she rarely did. She always moaned when I suggested a bath about lying in dirty water, but I always told her to have a shower first and then enjoy the hot water relaxing the body. She always tut-tutted and ignored my suggestion. That night, she didn't even bother with a shower but just got into the bath as it was filling. She had lit candles, and I just watched and listened to her make soothing sounds, not wanting to spoil her zen moment. I left her to watch the news, and after I had cleared the table, placed the dishes into the dishwasher and put the food from the kitchen into containers in the fridge. Tasneem was teaching me to cook, and I was quite good at making the basic dishes, but these days, neither of us cooked as we seemed to have a constant supply of food delivered to us by our families. My parents were visiting us over the coming weekend, and no doubt, there would be more dinners cooked; our fridge would be stocked up, and there would be plenty for sharing.

Tasneem did not come down, and I wondered if she had gone to bed. I went upstairs to check when she didn't reply to my call. We hated shouting at each other when in different rooms, and I thought that was why she did not reply to my calls from the bottom of the stairs. She wasn't in the bedroom. We only have a shower in our en suite bathroom, so I checked the family room and saw her, I thought, dozing in the bath. I asked her if she was all right, and she said she didn't feel well. I asked if she needed my help, and she asked me to give her a few minutes. Tasneem hated me seeing her pregnant and naked, even though I told her she looked beautiful all the time.

She managed to get out of the bath, came into the bedroom in her bathrobe and told me she felt very unwell. I asked her what she wanted me to do, and she said she just needed to rest. I went to prepare for bed, and she had managed to change into her night dress and get into bed, but she didn't look at all well. I got in and patted her hand. I read to Tasneem; she moved from her side to her back, then to the other side and was back on her back. She asked me to place pillows around her to see if this helped, but it did not. She was restless and not listening to me, so I asked her if she wanted me to put on some music which might help her relax and fall asleep, but she didn't want anything. She looked pale and uncomfortable, and I didn't know what to do to make it better.

I watched her starting to relax; she eventually fell asleep, and it didn't take me too long to fall asleep as well. I woke up about 3.30 am and found my bed empty. I found Tasneem pacing downstairs and the television on. I asked her if everything was okay and her look gave her away. She said she thought she still had months to go, but she thought she was having contractions, and as we talked, her waters broke. I asked her if we had got the dates wrong, but she shook her head as I watched a contraction ravaging her thin body. I asked her if she wanted me to call Tara or her mum, my mum. She shook her head. We had nothing ready; we were due to attend our first antenatal appointment next week and had decided that we would get a few basics for the baby after that. Unlike the baby shower, in the Sitabi we, as a community, are too superstitious to prepare and buy presents for the baby, instead only money is given to the mother. We hadn't toured the maternity ward yet and had made no decisions or plans about the birth, never mind buying so much as a nappy. It took all my effort not to panic; Tasneem was calmer than I would have been; I held her hand, and we tried to time her contractions; she asked me for her mobile phone, and I watched her dial one of her colleagues' mobile number. When there was an answer, she apologised for calling her at that time but was told straight away not to worry and how she could help. When Tasneem explained that her waters had broken, she was told not to panic. She had the phone on speaker, and I heard her being told to come into the hospital as soon as possible. I went and quickly dressed and got a small bag ready for Tasneem as she shouted instructions to me about what she needed me to pack for her. I would not have remembered the toiletries and her mobile charger. I wrapped her in a shawl, helped her into the back of the car and off we went. We were at our hospital in five minutes and in the maternity ward a few minutes later. I found a wheelchair and asked a porter to help us; he saw our staff passes, saw Tasneem and did not hesitate, knowing exactly what was needed. He wheeled us to the maternity ward and left us in Tasneem's friend's capable hands.

I was terrified and my insides were churning. I was so tired as Tasneem had been having restless nights over the last week, but here we were preparing her for birth. I wanted to call our families, but Tasneem refused to let me, telling me that birth took hours and why would we want to wake everyone in the middle of the night and worry them unnecessarily. She made me promise to wait until the morning to call both families, and I reluctantly agreed. We were in a private room; Tasneem was restless in bed and the midwife who attended her told her that she was 7 cm dilated, needed to be 10 cm and the birth would be soon and if she walked gently, then she might feel better and help the birth. Tasneem screamed with pain against her efforts to remain calm, and a doctor was called, who checked her and said that he was worried about the foetal heart rate and told Tasneem to lie down, and she was connected to a foetal monitor. I was so frightened, as they were with her; I snuck outside, called Tara and my parents.

When I entered the room moments later, I saw concern on all the faces and knew things were not going smoothly. I knew these looks very well. I wondered if they were thinking of a caesarean, but the doctor spoke to Tasneem and said he thought that the baby should come out now as he had an erratic heartbeat, bradycardia, but she was not dilated enough. They needed to slightly cut Tasneem to make room for the baby's head to come out, but it was too late to give her anaesthetic. Tasneem nodded, told them to do what was necessary and waited for the next contraction to pass. I held her hand and the doctor, midwife and other nurses who had come in to help did what they had to do. Tasneem's scream was primaeval but short and tears flowed from her eyes. She squeezed my hand so tightly I winced but did not pull away. I bent and kissed her forehead instead and then wiped her sweaty face with a damp cloth. It took them minutes to deliver the baby, and there was no cry. The baby was taken away and Tasneem asked me to go with him, but I was torn about what to do. She wriggled her hand out of mine and her eyes were clear in their instruction. Thank goodness, Tara arrived at that very moment and took over from me and told me to go so I got up and went to the incubator and watched them rubbing my baby, which looked no bigger than my hand, this skinny and tiny creature which looked human but made no sounds.

The midwife had her small finger in our baby's mouth and as she cleaned him, I heard a whimper, and they took the baby away to PICU, the baby intensive care unit. I was told the baby was fine, and I should go to Tasneem.

Tasneem was crying softly, and I thought my heart would break. I told her that our son was fine; they were just making sure, but they had not even thought to let her meet him. She said what if he died, and I told her to stop worrying, as soon as she had delivered the placenta, I would take her to see him. The next stages took ages, Tara's mum had entered the room, and it was a scene of chaos; Tasneem needed an injection, she had lost some blood and felt weak, but she said she was starving! She was crying and laughing. Tara told me to go and see what was happening to the baby. I left Tasneem in their safe hands and went to PICU. The nurses here really are angelic. Night shift for them is not sitting around in the quiet of the night, instead they were busy tending to about ten babies, checking each one, looking at monitors and writing notes for each. They recognised me and did not chide me, instead they showed me how I needed to dress in a gown, clean my hands and showed me my son. He was totally fine, but they were just checking him thoroughly as he had arrived so early and needed a bit of extra support. He lay naked, uncleaned and asleep. They told me that he was so tiny, they had placed him in an incubator so that he had similar conditions to the womb and would not go into shock as he was not yet fully developed. I nodded, not really listening to every single word being said to me. They said that I could sit and gently touch him if I wanted. I felt bad to do all this without Tasneem, but I did not hesitate and stood next to my son's incubator, stroking his tiny body with my hand through a hole at the side of the machine and feeling relief to see his tiny body breathing in and out on its own.

Tara and her mum arrived, but they were not allowed to enter the PICU. I loathed leaving our baby, but I knew they were worried, and I wanted to update them that our son was fine, he just needed extra care. I was torn between staying with him and going a few floors up to the birthing rooms to see Tasneem, and I would spend the next few days going back and forth between the two wards. I went to say goodbye to the baby and told him I would return shortly. I took some, well, rather a lot of photos, a couple of videos and showed them to everyone. We walked to Tasneem. She was now in the maternity ward; her face was full of worry and fear. I showed her the photos; she cried when she watched the videos, and I told her they would take her up to see him once she recovered herself. She needed a shower, and Tara said she would help her, and I went to find her breakfast as Tasneem told me she was close to fainting with hunger. She had had a cup of tea and some biscuits but was exhausted and starving. I nodded and kissed her on the lips, not caring who saw us. Tasneem's father and brother had just arrived and luckily brought a few things for her to eat and a flask of delicious chai for us both.

My parents arrived a few hours later. Tasneem could hardly keep her eyes open, but I knew she could not bear not seeing her son, so I let Tara and their mum take her to him in a wheelchair. Even after eating some toast, fruit and Indian snacks, she was very weak. We decided to go to PICU and see what was happening. We men stood admiring this tiniest of babies through the glass wall and none of us could hide our anxiety; Tasneem's father prayed, and we listened. I poured them some tea from a near-by machine, and we all bemoaned the fact that it was like drinking lukewarm water; the tea was so bad. I must remember to get some more chai for Tasneem. Tasneem was furious that no one had cleaned her baby, and she had made them let Tara and her mum enter, and they were gently cleaning our son with warm water and a soft cotton cloth. I was pleased as he really looked worst covered in all the birth fluids and bits of dried blood. The nurses tried to explain that they did not want the baby's temperature to drop, but the room was stifling hot, more like a sauna. Tasneem ignored their advice and made sure they thoroughly cleaned her baby and let her mother say the special prayers next to the baby's ears. We watched all this through the windows, and it was calming and beautiful to see. This baby knew he was loved and looked after from the second he was born.

We found my parents, Remi and Gulshan waiting for us at the maternity ward when we returned. As Tasneem was not there, they were told to wait outside the ward and I could see the worry on Mum's face. They all hugged Tasneem when she returned, then me and finally Tasneem's family. All laughed and cried and asked if the baby really was all right and were overjoyed to see the photos, videos, and I had to promise to forward these to each of them. Tasneem shared a room with two other mums and as we did not want to bother them; we took Tasneem to the family room. Remi had somehow managed to make some chapattis and a fresh coriander omelette with a flask of sweet, spicy chai at that time of the morning. We watched Tasneem eat a little; she was struggling to stay awake but loving the food. As the families chatted, I wheeled Tasneem to her room and helped her into her bed. She was in agony. She said that when she needed the toilet, it hurt so much, it made her cry, and she held her breath when she needed to pee as her inside stung with pain. She wanted to breastfeed and so had not been allowed any medication. She was mumbling; her eyes closed the minute her head was laid on the pillow and was fast asleep as soon as she lay down. I kissed her, covered her, tucked her in and left her after making sure again that she was settled in well.

My family again asked me if the baby really was well and I said I thought so, but we were waiting for a consultant to come and examine him. Remi gave me some chai and asked if I wanted any breakfast, but I thought I would throw it up if I ate any. I sipped the chai and let both my families pat me and reassure me that all would be well. We decided to go to the PICU and found that a nurse was coming to find me as the consultant paediatrician had arrived. She told me she was Tasneem's colleague and apologised for being late, but I was not worried about that, I just wanted to hear what she had to say. As there were so many people, she took us into a side room and I feared the worst. She smiled when she saw my look and told me there was nothing to worry about. She said that she thought that our baby was born about eight to ten weeks early. He was quite a long and tall little boy so looked very thin and was impatient to arrive into the world. He was healthy, but his internal organs were not yet fully developed, and it was best he stayed in an incubator for as long as necessary. They needed to give him an injection and needed my permission. I wondered if we needed to consult Tasneem, but she told me to let her sleep and rest as she had also gone through a massive event, plus the cut and blood loss. I nodded. All my family advised me to let the specialist do what was best for our son, and I nodded once I listened to what he needed and why. She told me I should go home and get some rest. I was loath to do this but knew I was getting tired and agreed to go home. We would take turns to stay with our new addition to our family and look in on Tasneem. Tasneem's mum wanted to stay; Tara was already sitting next to Tasneem, so I took my family to our home, and I left Tasneem's family looking after my son and wife.

We all slept. Gulshan had to shake me awake five hours later. My family had bought some tiny baby clothes, and Mum had packed a few more clothes for Tasneem as we were told she and our baby son would stay in hospital for a few weeks. I, too, was starving when I awoke; I had a shower just to wake me up fully and came downstairs to the wonderful smells of childhood. Remi and Gulshan had cooked lunch for Tasneem and her family. Poor Tasneem, she was to eat special food that would help her with milk production, food that would not hurt the baby and so there was little spice in her special food, just garlic, ginger with turmeric and fennel. There were lots of green herbs floating in what looked like a broth whilst we had normal, delicious and tasty spicy food. She got very annoyed two months later when she said she was bored of eating food that seemed to have only one flavour for lunch and dinner but learned quickly that if she deviated then she had a tiny baby boy who would squirm and whimper with wind and tummy ache.

We named our son Ismail, which means 'heard by Allah or God', on day six, the day of the naming ceremony. The customs involve a maternal aunt and sister carrying out various customs. The hospital had been amazing; they had found a private room for Tasneem, as there were so many women in and out of her shared rooms with different babies, that she never really got any rest. A portable incubator was installed next to Tasneem's bed. Ismail lay next to Tasneem's bed as we had decided with the expert to feed the baby on demand, which means feeding him any time he is hungry and this was all the time. Eventually, we had to give him top-up high protein feed especially late at night, only then would he sleep a few hours and this allowed Tasneem to rest and her body to stock up on more food to produce milk for our demanding son. The private room was a godsend; both families were able to squeeze into the room to watch the women carry out the naming ceremony. Tasneem dressed in clothes brought by my mum, Tara did her hair, painted her nails, and I was amazed to see Tasneem let her put on some make-up. There were special sweets made for Tasneem, rich in nuts, dried fruits and the usual spices like ginger and seeds rich in antitoxins and antiseptic properties. I tried them, and they were delicious. They helped Tasneem produce milk that did not hurt the baby but, instead, helped him build his immune system. All this made me appreciate our culture and traditions. It made me question my arrogance and previous haste to laugh at what I had thought of as silly superstitious and alternatives to medicine. I have a better understanding and appreciation now.

Having a baby did not stop us doing anything. Both our sons were easy children. Both had been born prematurely, a month early with our second son, and Tasneem laughed that they did this to cause her no birthing pain; they came within an hour or two after her waters had broken. I did not remind her of the fear and concern about Ismail's birth, her cut without anaesthetic and the intense pain she suffered at that time. It was better she had forgotten! Noor's birth was much more normal and straightforward. The babies were like us, impatient to enter the world and enjoy life as a family. Ismail was born with jaundice, but this is common in premature babies. Both of our sons spent a few weeks in hospital under light therapy in incubators to get rid of the excess bilirubin that caused the yellow jaundice colour in their skin and eyes. This time in the incubator allowed them to strengthen and develop their internal organs.

Both of our sons caught up quickly, and by the age of six months, they weighed the same as if they had been born to full term. Tasneem breast fed, but I topped these two insatiable babies with extra powdered milk formulae as our sons were always happy when they had full bellies. We were never short of babysitters, but on the whole, they came with us wherever we went. We never minded who carried and cuddled them; we never stopped people looking, touching and cooing over them. Our sons loved people; they were generally well behaved and liked people. The only time they got distressed was when they needed sleep, food or a nappy change, but they fell asleep easily if fed or held and noise did not bother them as we had never hidden them from everyday sounds, chatter and the constant clatter that happens in our family gatherings. I later became grateful that we were so open, honest and together as a united family. It helped me, my sons and Tasneem. It was what had willed me to live in those dark times when I was in a coma.

It took hard work for me to walk and talk after the knife attack. I was terrified of going back to work and wondered about seeing a therapist. At first, I consulted but did not start to do surgery until another year went by. I attended courses and retrained just to build my confidence and make sure I was safe to operate on patients. I had cuts to my hands and arms, but none had gone deep enough to damage any nerve endings. What the knifing had done was destroy my faith in my abilities, my confidence and I distrusted my skills. I had lost all credence in what I had always believed I had been good at.

My doubts subsided when my sons wrapped their arms around my legs or my neck, any feelings or fears I had of falling or tripping soon faded when tiny hands held mine or little arms tried to support my thin legs and willed me to walk. My sons were always clapping, whooped and shouted with joy at the tiniest progress I made. It was them who now watched, applauded and they even read to me stories of motivation, those with values and morals that encouraged me to push myself, never feel sorry, that made me laugh and chuckle.

The fear subsided after they imprisoned my attacker. The hospital suggested a conciliatory meeting; there was some scheme that suggested that if a victim met their perpetrator, shared feelings and told them about the harm they suffered, then it would help recovery. This made me furious. I never liked sob stories. Why did people not put effort into improving their abilities, why did they feel that using pity was a way to win a fight or earn a reward? I knew I was born with opportunities, but I always worked hard. I knew I was very lucky, but I am sure I could tell people stories that would make them feel compassion or cry, but I preferred to get people to trust me because of my learning, experience and skills in doing the best job possible. I refused to meet the perpetrator; I knew his beliefs and hatred of those who just looked different to him. I was no foreigner, yet he judged me negatively from the moment he saw me because I was a particular colour, culture and race. He refused to see my

Britishness. He had not changed and was criminalised again for these beliefs by being racist in another country. It was not my job to educate or forgive him; I wanted nothing from him. This man nearly killed me; he put Tasneem, my children and my family through terrible pain; they nearly lost me and, although I no longer blamed him, I did not want to be forced to have to forgive him. He was irrelevant to me. I stopped feeling the fear when I went back to the hospital to work. Tasneem and I talked about moving, leaving London, but I felt this was just another added punishment, we would lose being close to our families; we had such an easy life, and it took us a maximum of ten minutes to cycle to work. We liked the multicultural elements of London and this suited our children. Why should we be chased away?

I told Tasneem I would love a daughter. She nearly fell off her chair. She said that she thought we had decided on two children; our sons were now old enough to be more independent, and so why would I want to spoil this? I smiled and told her it was just a thought. She also laughed and said that we would probably have another son anyway had we tried!

Tasneem was pregnant two months later. She said that she was sure it was going to be another boy and I said, I thought so too but secretly continued to hope for a daughter and instead told Tasneem she would just have to keep trying until she gave me a daughter!

We called our third son Ayaan, which meant 'God's gift'. We did not have any more children after that. Instead we put our remaining energy into opening a paediatrics ward in two hospitals near Umayma's home in Malaysia. Tasneem and I took our sons to help set it up; we recruited specialists, surgeons and doctors in the UK and around the world to volunteer as much time as they could offer to work alongside Malaysian child specialists to learn from each other and help train to deliver some of the specialist care that saved Umayma's life. These hospitals were the two daughters Tasneem gave me, they were named 'Umayma' and 'Tasneem'. Both of our families visited Umayma and the hospitals over the years. The hospital links continue to this day. Tasneem's parents had never had the money to travel much before, but now that all the children were successful, married and their home had been paid for many years ago, they had the money and luxury of travel. After they completed the pilgrimage to Hajj, married off all their children, they started to travel, sometimes with us and at other times with each other only. They went back to India and even travelled there with my parents.

Tasneem and I visited Malaysia every other year with our children for the rest of our lives. We also went to India, to Uganda, back to Iran, Iraq, Egypt, we went around Europe with various families, to Central and South America. We always took our sons everywhere and they are as broadminded and adventurous as us. Ismail became a lawyer and works in human rights. Noor, our middle son, followed Tasneem's life path and spent two years working in one of the Malaysian hospitals as one of the top paediatric surgeons. He met and married a Malaysian, Ruqaiya, and they now live in the next street to us. Ayaan is the head of a primary school in Berkshire. All three sons are married and have their own children. Tasneem and I love being grandparents.